Cobra in My Kitchen
and Other Adventures with Wildlife

Stories * Poems * Essays

Zai Whitaker grew up in Mumbai, Maharashtra, in a family of naturalists, which was the beginning of her interest in wildlife and conservation. After college, she moved to Chennai, Tamil Nadu, and worked at the Madras Snake Park and later helped start the Madras Crocodile Bank near Mamallapuram, and the Irula Tribe Women's Welfare Society, Chengalpattu. She taught in Kodaikanal for 18 years and was the principal of two schools. She has written 20 books, most of them for young people, on environmental issues. These include *The Bird Man of India: Sálim Ali for Children* (Hachette India), *Andamans Boy*, *Sálim Mamoo and Me* and *Termite Fry*. She is the managing trustee of the Madras Crocodile Bank, where she lives.

Cobra in My Kitchen

and Other Adventures with Wildlife

Stories * Poems * Essays

Zai Whitaker

Illustrated by
Suddhasattwa Basu

hachette INDIA

First published in hardback in 2005 by Rupa Publications
7/16 Ansari Road, Daryaganj, New Delhi 110002

This edition published in 2024 by Hachette India
(Registered name: Hachette Book Publishing India Pvt. Ltd)
An Hachette UK company
www.hachetteindia.com

1

'Kali and the Rat Snake' and 'What Happened to the Reptiles' (in *Sorry Best Friend*) first published by Tulika Books, 305, Manickam Avenue, TTK Road, Alwarpet, Chennai 600018, Tamil Nadu, India.
'The Big Four' and 'Termite Safari' (titled 'On Safari') first published in *Chatterbox* magazine by Wheitstone Productions (P) Ltd., Bengaluru, India.
'The Zoo Tiger' first published in the *PC Magazine for Children*; 'How Scientists Can Affect the Crocodile's Love Life' first published in the *Indian Review of Books*; 'How to Fool Birdwatchers' adapted from Zai Whitaker's article first published in the *Birdwatcher's Newsletter*.

Old place names such as Calcutta, Bangalore, Trivandrum and Ooty, among others, have been used to preserve the historicity and historical authenticity of the text.

Subsequent edition/reprint specifications may be subject to change including but not limited to cover or inside finishes, paper, text colour and/or colour sections.

ISBN 978-93-5731-737-5

Hachette Book Publishing India Pvt. Ltd
4th & 5th Floors, Corporate Centre
Plot No. 94, Sector 44, Gurugram – 122003, India

Typeset by Manmohan Kumar, Delhi

Printed and bound in India
by Manipal Technologies Limited

MIX
Paper from responsible sources
FSC™ C043100

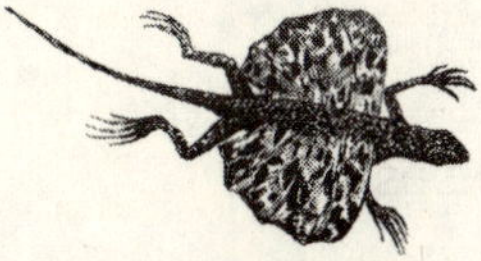

Contents

Cobra in My Kitchen

It was a rather hungry and foodless day, because there was a cobra in my kitchen. I wasn't keen on spending too much time there until it was removed...because it wasn't an ordinary, normal cobra – though that would have been bad enough – but a king cobra, one of the most dangerous snakes in the world. The fact that it was a baby, hatched that very day, didn't make it any better. Venomous snakes are venomous from birth, and to make it even more uncomfortable, there was no king cobra antivenom in India then. (Even now, the only king cobra antivenom one can get is from Thailand, and more suitable against the king cobras there.)

This one had hatched, along with its 20 brothers and sisters, in a large bread box with holes for air, and a cushioning of soil and leaf humus. The eggs had been collected from a wild nest in the Andaman Islands.

The bread box had been sitting on the bookshelf in our living room for a month. We'd woken up to find that they'd hatched...and several had managed to squeeze through the holes and were happily roaming around the house. All the others had been caught, but this kitchen one obviously liked it there, and had found a good hiding place.

How, and why, on earth was I in this ridiculous situation? How did I end up in this snaky sort of life? All through school and college I'd dreamed of various careers I wanted for myself: teaching, journalism, dressmaking and cooking, among others. And, oh yes, most of all I wanted to be a translator or interpreter. I liked the idea of sitting importantly in those United Nations conferences with earphones draped over my head. Once, I even had a brief ambition to be a doctor, but it quickly left me when I discovered that it meant five years of serious study.

In the middle of all this, while I was studying German to start my great United Nations career, I met and married Rom Whitaker. I moved to Chennai (then Madras) and began working with him at the Snake Park, which he had started some years earlier. And that's why there was a king cobra in my kitchen. It was only the next morning that it was discovered in a mixing bowl and taken away to the park in disgrace.

For the next eight or nine years, the Snake Park was the centre of my life. It was very different from what it is today. There were fewer buildings, and more greenery and open space. The office was a small, thatched house with a tree growing in the courtyard. The large central 'pit' or open enclosure had three or four hundred snakes and lizards of many different species. Visitors loved walking slowly round it, spotting snakes in the low bushes, or in the pools of water, or on the ground. Sometimes there would be large rat snakes curled up in the branches of a tree, or a monitor lizard sitting on a log, calmly looking around for a frog to snack on. Often a bunch

of 20 or 30 watersnakes would get together for a soak in the pool, only their heads sticking out like the hydra of Greek mythology. A visitor would jump back in fright as a cobra flashed its hood in defence, expanding its ribs to display the spectacle markings. You could hear the calls of toads and frogs as they were caught by a snake. Visitors often spent an hour or more here, watching the activities of these beautiful creatures.

The most popular, of course, were the cobras and large rat snakes, some of them over two metres long. The bright green vine snakes with their pointed heads and strange eyes, and the fast bronzeback tree snakes, were also favourites. Snake Park staff would get into the pit now and then, pick up a harmless keelback or vine snake, and let visitors hold it.

There were large, landscaped, glass-fronted cages with interesting and famous snakes from India as well as abroad – African puff adders, American rattlesnakes and Japanese habus. There was a display of the Big Four dangerous snakes of India, about which I have written in a separate chapter ('The Big Four') in this book. A family of marsh crocodiles, a pair of giant tortoises from the Seychelles islands, sea snakes and a group of big water monitor lizards, were also residents of the park. The location was beautiful, as it was a part of Guindy Deer Park, with evergreen shrubs, beautiful old trees, and cheetal and blackbuck wandering around.

Our job at the Snake Park was to make people feel a little more friendly towards snakes. In India, snakes are often killed on sight. All snakes are considered dangerous. Strange and frightening stories are told and retold (and believed!) about how monstrous snakes can be. People go to great trouble and expense to clear the land around their homes to keep snakes away. Some feel ill, and even develop a fever, when they see a snake.

I had always known about this general fear of snakes (I myself was not too happy in the presence of snakes), but working at the Snake Park opened my eyes to the national hysteria about these poor reptiles. My special job was to write and distribute factual information about snakes and snakebite.

How do you fill a snake park with snakes? And frogs and rats for them to eat? It's not an easy business, and it was possible only because of the Irular tribe of snake catchers, which lives on the outskirts of Chennai. The Irular are hunter-gatherers famous for their snake tracking and catching skills. They were the main suppliers of animals to the park, and soon after coming to Chennai I saw their jungle talents at work. We went on a cobra-finding mission with Natesan, an old hunter with the long, tangled hair and sun-beaten face of true jungle people.

The rains had started, and the soft ground made tracking easy. Tracking snakes, however, requires extraterrestrial vision of some sort. Being light and fast, snakes leave almost invisible scrapes on the ground, which only the Irular are able to spot and 'read'.

Leaving the jeep near a small Irular hamlet about 30 kilometres from the city, we followed Natesan through a patch of scrub forest and out into bright green rice fields. We must have walked for about 15 minutes when Natesan slowed down, pointed to an invisible (to us) mark in the soil, and followed the track to a nice big rat hole partly hidden by a thorn bush.

'Cobra,' he announced briefly.

'How do you know?' we asked, feeling quite foolish as we always did when out with the Irular.

Natesan just smiled and squatted by the hole. This hole, he explained after some time, was the home of a gerbil, a pretty, acrobatic rodent that the Irular eat. Yes, rats are often on the menu and a curry made of clean field rats is tasty and full of protein. Snakes, he said, often moved into rat holes (after eating the occupant), as this one obviously had.

Natesan started working at the hole with his crowbar, alternately digging and scooping away the soil. Every now and then he would stop to read signs that told him which way the tunnel turned. At one point he reached out to a bush, snapped off a green twig, and pushed it into the tunnel, watching it carefully. It didn't move; which meant it hadn't touched the snake, which meant the snake was deeper down and more digging was to be done. It was jungle technology at its best. Dig, dig, dig, a little to the left, then to the right, then straight down, and the twig is inserted again. Wow, it gives a big jerk, as if a cobra had nudged it in irritation.

Two or three more thrusts of the powerful muscle-propelled tool and the cobra springs out, taking all of us by surprise. It was over a metre long, fat and shiny and full of pep. Wild or freshly caught cobras look very different from the sick, de-fanged animals which snake charmers use. This one had shed its skin recently and its colours were bright and fresh, as if newly painted.

After admiring it for a while, Natesan 'pinned' the head: he used his crowbar to gently press the head to the ground and controlled the thrashing body with his foot. Quickly grabbing the neck with one hand and the tail with the other, Natesan stood there calmly, as if catching a cobra was an everyday matter. Depositing the snake in a cotton 'snake bag' – about the size of a pillowcase – he knotted the top and tucked it into the waist of his *veshti*. Many an Irular has been bitten this way, because snake fangs can easily penetrate the thin cotton layers, but it's a convenient way of transporting snakes, and old habits die hard!

By midday Natesan had quite a collection: striped keelbacks, vine snakes, two cobras and a young monitor lizard. Now, he said, he was hungry and would concentrate on rats for a while. And he was lucky, because under a low, scrubby bush he spotted the burrow of a family of gerbils. This species of rodent lives in a veritable maze of burrows, one leading into another, providing many good hiding places in case of a predator attack. The ground area of the entire 'compound' could be up to five or six square metres!

With this kind of architecture, digging was out of the question and Natesan fell back on the 'smoking' technique. Getting out a small earthen pot that Irular often carry with them, he filled it with dry twigs, and lit it. Natesan placed the mouth of this blazing inferno over one of the burrow entrances and blew into a small hole on the other side. Smoke billowed into the network of tunnels, suffocating the inhabitants. A few managed to escape, though Natesan had armed us with sticks and instructions to whack any runaways. But chasing a bouncing gerbil through thorny scrub forest isn't easy.

We were soon chomping on our prey, delicately roasted on an open fire. Not something I would choose to have every day, but pretty good when you're starving and it's the only item on the menu. I was the only one picking at it hesitantly. The others were gorging themselves as if they were at Kentucky Fried Chicken. I might have done the same if I hadn't known what I was eating.

The Snake Park was becoming a popular tourist attraction. It was also a meeting point for scientists and naturalists – or just ordinary people interested in reptiles. We received letters from all over the country, giving us information or asking questions. Through our many correspondents we learned facts new to science: for example, a particular snake was found in a previously unknown habitat, or the food of a snake or lizard included an unrecorded item. To keep these friends and well-wishers of the Snake Park informed about the goings-on there, I started a little newsletter called *Hamadryad*, which is another name for the king cobra. Now our cobweb of communication grew even bigger; there were reptile people in Bangladesh, Nepal, Sri Lanka, Malaysia and other neighbouring countries who wrote to us regularly. Opening the mail every morning was an exciting business; sometimes, a bulky envelope would turn out to have a shed snakeskin, or, once, even the dried faeces of some reptile!

We were also finding out how little was known about Indian reptiles, and how much work needed to be done in this field. The research wing of the Snake Park grew, concentrating on endangered species like king cobras, various turtles and tortoises, and crocodiles. I was able to take part in some of the studies and surveys, and there were many adventures, both good and bad.

One year, we took a motorbike on a boat across to Sri Lanka, and criss-crossed the southern part of that country looking for crocodiles. We camped on the River Karnali in Nepal, observing the gharial. We visited a temple tank in Tripura where turtles are considered holy, and are fed and cared for. Some of these experiences are written about in this book.

Come along with me!

Serpentine Mythsss

As soon as people start talking about snakes, all kinds of myths and stories begin. India is as full of snake myths as it is of snakes. For example, people swear that snakes drink milk...and you can't convince them that they don't, because these are 'facts' that have been handed down from generation to generation.

So, one morning, a van drove up to the Snake Park with two large steel cans, the kind used for transporting milk. Each one must have had at least 30 litres of milk. A lady came into the office to say that this was part of a family *puja*, and they wanted to donate the milk for the snakes. We tried to tell her that snakes don't drink milk, where would a snake get milk in the wild, and that their natural food is frogs, rats, birds and other small animals...but she was determined to carry out her *puja*, and was quite sure that snakes drink milk. Not wanting to come in the way of her religious rituals, we finally took it and distributed it to the staff after she left. Everyone had a milk feast and took large bottles of it home with them.

Another time, a deaf lady was brought to the park for a cobra-tail treatment. Again, no one had the heart to say it wasn't going to work. A cobra was caught, and its tail pushed into the lady's ears, one after the other, and kept there for a few minutes. Needless to say, she didn't start hearing again, even though the treatment was repeated several times.

Another colourful but untrue snake story is that if you kill a snake, its mate will take revenge. How is this possible, when snakes have tiny, simple brains that are only capable of 'thoughts' about eating, resting,

shedding skin and other such activities? Revenge is a human emotion, and does not feature in the world of animals. Thank goodness for that; otherwise, animals would be after our blood all the time, since we do so much harm to them!

Other snake myths that are commonly believed are that rat snakes mate with cobras, that they slash paddy plants with their tails, that the green vine snake (which has a pointed head) will peck at your eyes, that sand boas have two heads, and that the bronzeback tree snake will bite someone, then climb a high tree to wait for the victim's funeral! People also believe that cobras have a precious jewel in their head. If this were true, then poor snake-catcher tribes like the Irular of Tamil Nadu would be rich!

A frequent discussion with visitors was whether snakes can hear or not. Yes, they can, everyone said, because they dance to the music of the snake charmer's flute. No-no, we'd counter, they're following the movements of the flute and not its music. But it's not easy to wipe out generation-long stories and beliefs, and sometimes we just gave up. Until 1991, when snake charmers were banned, they made good use of people's ignorance about snakes. Making the cobra 'dance' to the music of the flute, they earned a good living.

Many non-venomous snakes like the python and rat snake are believed to be dangerous. This leads to a fear of all snakes. People faint after being bitten by a harmless, non-venomous snake, from sheer shock and fright. Although the only cure for snakebite is antivenom, there are many dangerous beliefs about the treatment of snakebite. You can actually buy a 'snake stone', which is supposed to draw out snake venom from your blood after a bite.

Then there are the snakebite 'healers' who chant mantras and prayers, or give you 'medicines'. One of the strangest types of 'healers' were the telegram-doctors, many of them station masters, who cured snakebite without even seeing the patient. Magic! All you had to do is send him a telegram (an urgent postal message). The magic mantras he then sang were supposed to cure you in a few minutes!

There are many more stories about snakebite cures like these. And people swear that they have seen them work 'with their own eyes'. Even a college professor once said that his friend was bitten by a cobra, and cured with a snake stone.

He said his friend was fine after half an hour of the treatment. What's the explanation?

The fact is that not every venomous snakebite is fatal, or capable of killing the bitten person. A certain

percentage, quite a high number actually, of snakebites will not harm us because too little – or no – venom has been injected by the snake. A study done on cobra bites showed that only ten per cent are dangerous. In most cases, therefore, the patient will survive anyway, whether he uses a snake stone, goes to a quack doctor, sends a telegram or does absolutely nothing. The same principle is true for all species: the snake doesn't know how much venom it needs to put into you, nor is it interested in killing you. It feels attacked and threatened, and wants to get away as soon as possible.

Typically, the bite happens when a person steps on a snake in the dark. But dangerous bites, where enough venom has been injected to harm you, have to be treated with antivenom. Since we can't judge or measure how much venom has gone in, it is best not to take a chance, and go straight to the hospital for treatment.

Another common Indian myth about reptiles is that some lizards are poisonous. One of these is the monitor lizard which is called *goh-saamp* and another is the leopard gecko of north India. Its local name is *hun khun*, which means 'kill and take'. The harmless gecko is supposed to be dangerous; people say that if you eat food in which a gecko has fallen, you can get very sick and even die. This, of course, is not true. There are no poisonous lizards in India, and only two in the world. These are far, far away in the USA and Mexico.

Reptiles play a big part in Hindu mythology and folklore. The *nagas*, or cobras, are the rulers of the underworld, which overflows with jewels and gems and other wealth. Perhaps this is why people believe that cobras have a gem in their head. The *naga* rulers have five, seven, or nine hoods, and represent eternity. They are often shown with their tail in their mouth, a symbol of timelessness. The king of the *nagas* is called Ananta, which means 'unending'. Ananta is often shown with the god Vishnu, who sometimes rests on him. The snake's nine hoods, spread wide like umbrellas, protect Vishnu's head.

The snake god Ananta was with Vishnu during his incarnation as Krishna. The story is that one stormy night, baby Krishna had to be taken across a river to safety, and Ananta protected him with his nine hoods. There is a similar story about Lord Buddha, who was protected during a storm by the hooded serpent Muchalinda.

Ananta remains by Vishnu's side throughout the many destructions and creations of the world. He supports the world and the heavens with his hoods, while sitting on the back of a tortoise. This is why some temples have a carving of a tortoise on the floor, on which many tourists must have stumbled. But Vishnu's official carrier is the divine eagle-like bird Garuda, the enemy of snakes. Garuda, of course, has a magical power against snake venom. In the past, in the town of Puri in Odisha, people bitten by snakes were sometimes taken to a special temple pillar carved in the shape of Garuda and made to cling to it in the belief that it would prevent the venom from taking effect.

Our mythology is full of stories of fights between the *naga*s and Garuda. Once, the serpents captured Garuda's mother and took her away to the underworld. They then demanded, as ransom, a cup of *amrit*, the nectar of immortality. Garuda went off to get it, but as he was handing it to the serpents, another god ran off with it. Some of the snakes, however, managed to lick a few drops that fell to the ground, and became immortal. The power of the drink made a cleft, or split, in their tongues. This is why snakes have forked tongues.

Another famous serpent in Indian mythology is Kaliya. Now, Kaliya was a wicked snake, a demon really, with ten heads, and he lived in a river. His poisonous breath destroyed everything around him.

But the child Krishna wasn't afraid of him, and danced on his heads and overpowered him.

Then there are the three snakes that twine themselves around Shiva. One above his head, one round his neck, and the third round his waist. Even Shiva's earrings are snakes.

I have talked so much about snakes that there is little space left for the other reptiles in our mythology. But I cannot end without a mention of Makara, the crocodile on which Varuna, the god of the seas, rides. Makara has a deer's head and antelope legs. Sometimes, though, it is also shown as a perfectly normal crocodile. The word 'mugger' (or *magar*), Hindi for crocodile, comes from the Sanskrit '*makara*'.

So many wonderful stories! Perhaps that's why people are so afraid of reptiles: because they have done wonderful and terrible things in our myths and legends. However, it is important to separate these from the real facts about them, and remember that they are harmless, useful animals that are more frightened of us than we are of them.

The Big Four

One summer I was on a beach near Mumbai. We cousins were sitting around boasting about our adventures that day. One cousin had stolen mangoes from an aunt's garden, another had 'borrowed' an uncle's car and gone for a spin around the countryside, a third (me) had sneaked away to the Big Banyan while the grown-ups were sleeping.

'And on the way, at the water tank, what do you think I saw?'

Everyone looked at me expectantly.

I enjoyed the attention, and announced, 'A snake. A big watersnake.'

'Did you kill it?' asked the cousins.

This was the moment I was waiting for. I had become interested in snakes and took every opportunity to preach about how useful they were, and how they shouldn't be killed. I was getting famous in our family as the great Protector of Snakes. It felt good. 'Kill it? Why on earth?' I retorted. 'Don't you guys know that snakes eat rats and are very good for the environment, and also that most snakes are not venomous? Snakes have a right to be around, just like other animals.'

Just then we heard a strange sound. Like a small steam engine, or like air being let out from one of those blow-up toys. Or maybe a passing truck having a bad attack of puncture. Running out and looking around, we discovered it was none of these, but a large Russell's viper sitting in a bush, speaking its mind. It wasn't happy at all. Neither was I. I wished I hadn't spoken like a protector of snakes. The cousins looked at me, waiting for me to do something. It was awful.

'Will you catch it?' a cousin asked. I tried to look brave, like a snake catcher. But fortunately, the snake came to my rescue and suddenly shot off into the vegetation and disappeared. I got brave once more. 'Just as well,' I said, 'I hate keeping snakes in captivity.'

Just then the gardener and his son came running up with a big stick and began poking about, looking for the snake and making loud hunting sounds. I began my Snake Protector speech all over again. But the gardener had no time for all that. 'Madam,' he said, 'you sleep on a bed, in a room, safe from snakes. But we sleep on the ground, in the open, during the hot months.'

I felt very small. He was absolutely right. It's one thing to be indoors at night and another to be sharing ground space with snakes. I was still glad the Russell's viper had escaped, but began to understand the village person's fear of snakes. After all, over 50,000 people die of snakebite every year in India. Most of these deaths are caused by four common dangerous snakes, often called the Big Four: cobra, krait, Russell's viper and saw-scaled viper.

Although there are many more venomous snakes in India – about 50 out of 350 species – only these

Cobra

Krait

four are medically important, causing the majority of deaths. Some, like pit vipers, have a very mild venom that is not capable of killing a person. Others, like the king cobra, live in habitats where you and I are not likely to go, such as thick rainforest. And yet others, like the banded krait, are gentleman-snakes: they simply don't like to bite. (The ready-biters, like the Russell's viper, should learn a lesson from them.)

The most famous of the Big Four is, of course, the cobra, which used to be the snake charmer's tool. As mentioned earlier, the cobra wasn't happily dancing to the sound of the *been*, the traditional flute used by the snake charmers. What we were seeing was a sick animal with its fangs pulled out or mouth sewed up, terrified out of its wits. It never survived long because it couldn't eat.

Cobras are much more beautiful in their natural setting: fields and forests. They eat mostly rats, mice and frogs, and are nocturnal (moving around at night). The Russell's viper and saw-scaled viper – though both vipers – are easy to tell apart. The Russell's is large and heavy, growing to a metre in length. The saw-scaled is small but compensates for its size by running its saw-edged scales together to make a loud 'hiss'. A proper snake hiss is supposed to come from the mouth, but this snake doesn't follow the rules. Both these vipers are rodent eaters, and are commonly found on the borders of fields, where rats are plentiful. Vipers have a haemotoxic venom, which means it affects the

Russell's viper

blood. The long, curved fangs of the Russell's viper are capable of giving a powerful injection, and are certainly a great rat-catching tool. Within seconds, the prey is paralyzed by this natural syringe.

Krait venom, like that of the cobra, is neurotoxic, or nerve-affecting. Kraits are blue-black, usually with thin white cross-bands on the back. They like nightlife, and move around quietly after dark, looking for prey (rats and mice). Many krait bites happen at night, when people are sleeping outside and flick at the snake in their sleep, thinking it must be an insect. They often don't realize they've been bitten because neurotoxins don't bring on symptoms quickly. This also means the victim may not get the antivenom in time.

All this talk of venom, and bites, and deaths, is scary, isn't it? But we have to remember that road accidents and dog bites cause many more deaths than snakebites do. We have to learn certain 'tricks' to avoid getting bitten, that's all.

The first is, don't put your hand or leg into a bush or grass patch unless you can see it is snake-less. Snakes can lie very still, and look like twigs/branches/ropes. Second, use a bright flashlight at night; it is easy to step on a 'twig' and get bitten. Third, if you DO get bitten, stay calm. There is a big chance that it isn't a venomous snake. There is also a big chance that even if it is, it didn't give you enough venom to do any harm ('dry' bites are common). And last – but not least – go to the hospital anyway. Just in case it is a venomous snake and it did decide to inject enough venom, you will need antivenom serum. I repeat, this is the ONLY medicine for snakebite, so don't go off towards snake stones and mantras and other 'cures'.

Sometimes, we don't like someone too much, but we learn to live with them. It's the same with snakes. Snakes and people are kind of stuck with each other. And we have to remind ourselves that if there were no snakes, the world would be overrun with rats. Rats in food, rats on our beds, rats on the roof. And rats generously spread disease, such as plague and leptospirosis. I'd much rather have a few snakes running around, wouldn't you?

Saw-scaled viper

Jungle Holidays

Most honeymooning couples go to places like Goa or Ooty* and stay in five-star hotels. They wear beautiful clothes, smile at each other, take photographs, and share everything, even riding the same horse and munching the same *bhutta*. They take bites from each other's plates, sip each other's drinks, and giggle and whisper a lot. I was really looking forward to my honeymoon.

However, my honeymoon turned out to be rather different, mainly because I had married a sort of Tarzan. He felt that the biggest treat he could offer me was not the Taj or West End hotels, but the jungle. Two days after the wedding, I found myself bumping along in a jeep on a forest road in Wayanad, Kerala. It was raining hard and the canvas flaps of the jeep couldn't keep

*Short for Udhagamandalam

the water out. I was soon drenched, and so was my suitcase filled with silk saris and matching jewellery.

'You're just going to love this place,' said Rom enthusiastically.

I tried to look excited and happy – not very successfully. It didn't matter though, because he wasn't noticing anything but the forest sights and sounds.

Our drive came to an end where a large tree had fallen across the track. 'That's okay, we can walk from here,' said my newly acquired husband cheerfully. Jumping out into the pelting rain, he looked down and pointed excitedly at a yellowish cake of dung. 'Elephants! Quite recent too. And – oh, wow! Leeches. See that? And that? See 'em?'

Now let me go back a little and tell you how the two of us met. The common thread in our lives was wildlife. My father was a naturalist, and that was how Rom came into my life. Like him, I loved the forest, and animals and birds. Together, we had done shows on wildlife for schoolchildren. We had written letters to politicians about saving forests that were about to be cut down for timber or hydroelectric dam projects. We had gone birdwatching together, read the same books about ecology and animal studies. I had even made a little butterfly collection to impress my husband-to-be.

But hey, come on. It's one thing to catch butterflies and know the names of a few plants and animals and another altogether to find yourself in elephant country, surrounded by leeches eagerly inching towards your feet.

Yet, sometimes you simply don't have a choice. After all, I had happily agreed to visit this forest when Rom had described it. 'Sounds fantastic!' were my own foolish words. So there I was, wrapped in a plastic sheet, knapsack on my back, following him down the muddy, slippery trail dotted with elephant dung.

'How far is it?' I asked, trying to sound casual.

'Not far. Just a bit more.'

That walk almost killed me. My shoes were too fashionable and too tight, my knapsack too heavy. Soon he was carrying it, and I was limping as secretly as possible. We were on our way to a large rock, accommodation which Rom had used several months earlier while on a snake-catching trip.

It turned out to be a six-hour walk, and it was dusk before we arrived at the rock on a stream bank. It was in a slight depression, and I named it Honeymoon Hole (but didn't tell him). On the far side was a lovely little waterfall above a grassy slope with more elephant droppings. I sat down to recover while he cooked dinner and organized camp. At night, the clouds rushed away as the wind picked up. Millions of bright stars filled the sky. Far away, there was a rather panthery sound, and I recalled Ogden Nash:

> 'Should you behold a panther crouch,
> Prepare to say ouch;
> Better yet if called by a panther –
> Don't anther.'

Three days at Honeymoon Hole taught me a lot. I learnt that elephants don't spend their time looking for humans to terrorize; they actually move away when they sense human presence. I learnt that sitting on a grassy bank with your feet in a cold stream and the sun on your back is one of the most wonderful experiences in the world. I learnt that every forest noise doesn't mean danger. And, best of all, I learnt that leeches don't like rocks. I never really became a 'jungle girl'...but I did start enjoying our jungle trips. Especially after they were over.

A few months later we were in the Ashambu Hills. Once more, we were on our way to a favourite rock. But this time we got lost getting to it. By nightfall, we were in an abandoned cardamom plantation about two kilometres south of our destination. We decided to dine at a nearby stream and then carry on with the help of our powerful flashlight. Dinner consisted of two small cubes of rubbery matter. This was a present from a Japanese friend – survival rations prepared for the Japanese army, which included all the minerals and nutrients our body needs in a day. It was a good lesson in the difference between food and nutrition. How I longed for a plate of hot rice and dal!

Time to move on; Rom extracted the flashlight from his knapsack and switched it on. Dark as ever. It must have clicked on in the bag because the battery was dead. No amount of shaking, hitting and cursing was of any help. We ended up doing a sort of Olympic relay with a flaming branch, singing tunelessly to warn the animals of our nervous arrival.

The campsite was spectacular; but, once again, dotted with elephant dung. At dawn, we were woken up by the honking of hornbills as a pair flew overhead. While brushing our teeth, three dholes or wild dogs turned the corner, whistled to one another in alarm and trotted away. We always kept a night-fire going to tell the animals that we were in residence.

I discovered some months later that sleeping in elephant country is easier than sleeping on a

crocodile, which is what we had to do, to prevent its escape. It was on the banks of a large dam in the Nilgiri foothills, and we were collecting crocodile eggs to take back and hatch in Chennai. It had been an incredibly lucky trip. We'd found one nest on the verge of hatching. As we tapped the earth covering of the nest, a chorus of ready-to-hatch crocodiles answered with their eager *nyuk*, *nyuk*, *nyuk*.

Further up the river, we'd seen fresh tracks of a crocodile going down a tunnel through a tangle of banyan roots. Rom wanted to put an identity tag on it, but it was too dark to get out our nets and catch it. So we slept on the tunnel like prison guards. It was an interesting and, for me, rather sleepless night.

On another croc trip, in Nepal this time, we camped on the River Karnali while Rom studied the small population of gharial. With us was a group of Norwegian engineers who were soon to start building a disastrous dam across the river. The place was overrun by scorpions and almost every night one of us 'got the treatment'. The Karnali Gorge, just upriver from our camp, is surely one of the most beautiful places on earth. Most evenings, a panther called from across the river. The cowherds would sing long, wonderful ballads on their way home in the evening.

It's good therapy to exchange one's roof for the stars every once in a while. You always come back prepared for another dose of life.

Kali and the Rat Snake

Kali walked along the thorny forest track. As slowly as he could. He was on his way to school.

Kali's father was one of the most famous snake catchers of the Irular tribe. He had caught over a hundred cobras this monsoon and bought many good things for the family. The snake cooperative paid Rs 150 for each venomous snake. They took out the venom from snakes to make antivenom. When Kali went snake-catching with his father, his legs worked like machines. But now he dragged his feet.

'I hate school,' he told the bushes as his walk got slower and slower, 'and school hates me.' The bushes did not seem to understand or feel sorry for him. 'It's been two months since I joined school, but I don't have a single friend. I get the feeling...I think they think we Irular are weird.'

On the first day of school, each student had to stand up and tell the class three things: his or her name, the name of the village, and what their father did. 'My name is Ramu, my village is Meloor, my father is a bus conductor,' said the first child. Then came 'Selvi, Orathur, postman.'

When it was Kali's turn, he was so proud he felt like a balloon. 'I am Kali, my village is Kanathur, my father is a snake catcher.' The children giggled and nudged one another as if he'd said something silly. For the first time in his life, Kali did not feel proud of being an Irular. He wished he were just like the others – an ordinary boy with a bus-conductor father. Anyway, that was two months ago. Kali was getting used to it but it was hard. And his school walk got slower and slower.

Kali reached the school gate as the bell was ringing. As usual, he sat in the back row. Alone. Wishing he had friends. Wishing he could fail and be thrown out of school. But failing wasn't easy. He had tried. But however badly he wrote his lessons, the teacher seemed pleased with him.

This morning they had maths and writing, and then it was break-time. The children rushed outside to have their snacks. Some had *idli*, others had mixture, a slice of bread, or two or three biscuits. Kali opened

his tiffin box. Oh no! Fried termites! His favourite actually, but what if someone saw?

He'd have to hide. He sat on the wall, far away from the others, and finished his tiffin. Termites didn't taste as good here as they did at home. 'Suppose someone comes near me? Suppose someone asks what I've brought?' Kali wondered anxiously.

The bell rang. Break was over. It was the same teacher but another subject – English. They had to write the English alphabet on their slates. Teacher walked around the room with a stick, bringing it down sharply on the desk of a child who had made mistakes. 'Lucky,' thought Kali. Lucky that he could make the teacher angry! He would try and make a mess of his slate too.

Teacher stood in front of Kali. But instead of a swish of the stick, he got a pat on the back. Teacher held up Kali's slate for the class to see. 'Here! This is the sort of work I want to see from everyone,' he said.

Now the others would hate him more than ever. Kali could hear the whispering in the classroom. He'd never have friends in school. And he'd never get kicked out.

Just then, something happened in the room. At first Kali didn't understand. Arms and legs flew. Bodies ran, tumbled over each other, fell, ran some more. There were shouts from all directions. 'Help! Help! Teacher, help!' But the teacher was under his table. Eyes and hands pointed to the ceiling. Now Kali understood.

There on the roof was a large rat snake. It must have smelt rats on the roof tiles and come after them. By mistake, it had taken a wrong turn and come to class instead.

Kali's father said that sometimes snakes smelt humans and mistook them for rats. Maybe this one thought, 'Wonderful, here's a roomful of rats!' The rat snake was wrapped around a palmyra beam on the roof. It stretched out its neck curiously. It must have been surprised by all the excitement. Slowly, more

and more of its body uncoiled from the beam. Kali, looking up, knew what was going to happen next. And it did.

Dhopp! Down fell the rat snake. The noise and confusion grew worse. Chairs crashed. Heads banged. Bodies hit the wall, the floor, one another. Teacher was now on, not under, his table, yelling 'Save me! Save me!'

The rat snake was terrified. It went to one side of the room, then the other. The children ran in the opposite direction.

For a few seconds Kali was too surprised to do anything. His people, the Irular, always went towards snakes, not away from them. Had everyone gone mad? He walked slowly to where the snake was. He reached out his hand. Suddenly, the room grew still. No sound, no

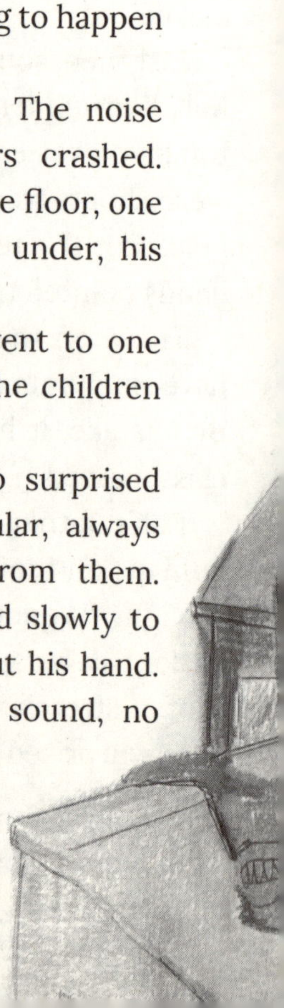

movement. All eyes were on Kali. The rat snake – it was over two metres long – reared back like a horse, opened its mouth wide, hissed and struck. Luckily, it missed Kali's hand.

'The bite of a big rat snake is very painful.' This was the thought that went through Kali's mind as he grabbed the snake behind the head. His other hand gripped the long muscular body. Soon, Kali was all wrapped up in snake.

Kali thought he would find a big bag to put the rat snake in. He'd take it home to Father. The Vandalur Zoo near Chennai paid a good price for rat snakes. He'd buy his baby sister a new dress... But what was this noise? What was happening? Was there another snake in the room? Confused, Kali looked up.

Everyone clapped and cheered. And then they chanted: 'Ka-li! *Nand-ri*! Ka-li! *Nand-ri*! Ka-li! Thank-you!' It was so wonderful. Kali's eyes soon became wet with happiness. He grinned and the clapping grew louder.

'You saved us!' shouted one of the boys. 'How brave you are!'

'From now on, you sit next to me!'

'No, me!'

And the children started quarrelling about whom Kali would sit next to. 'Who taught you to be so brave?' asked Ramesh, the class bully. 'Come on, name it. We'll give you whatever you want; you saved our lives.'

'Well, what I want now,' replied Kali, 'is a bag. A big one. To put this fellow into.'

Ten children ran off in ten different directions to find bags. The others looked at Kali with admiration.

From the corner of his eye, Kali saw Teacher climb down from his desk.

Teacher walked up to Kali, but he was careful not to get too close. 'Silly children!' he scolded. 'Why did you get so scared? Running all over the place just because of a non-venomous snake!'

Teacher walked back to his desk. As soon as his back was turned, Kali and the children grinned at one another. Secret grins, the kind that friends use.

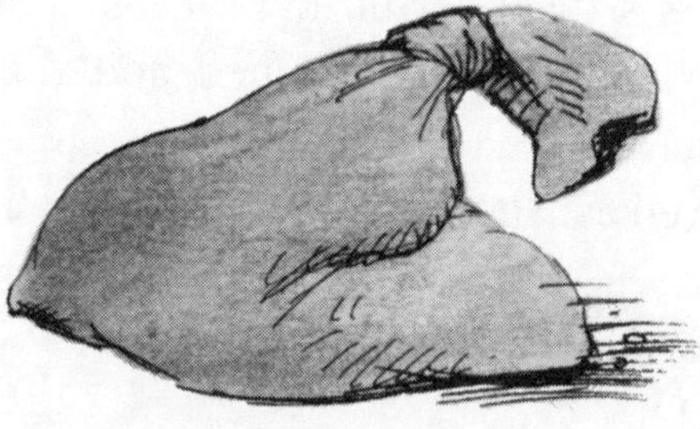

Snakes Are Decent

Snakes are decent, they're all right –
They don't really mean to hiss and bite...
But remember that snakes
Can make mistakes,
And also remember
That, in a temper,
They can give you an enormous fright.

Leave Your Tail and Run!

(How Reptiles Defend Themselves)

It's probably not much fun being a small reptile – snake, lizard, crocodile, turtle or tortoise. Because you always have to be alert for predators. A young crocodile, for example, can be gobbled up by birds, jackals, frogs, big fish, big crocodiles, turtles, man... to name a few. Not much time to relax, and a lot of worries. How can a small animal defend itself against a much, much larger predator? It would be ridiculous for a tree snake to pretend it could fight off an eagle, or for a skink to believe it could overpower a crocodile. So the next best thing is to bluff and trick your way through life, and reptiles are very good at this.

When a cobra spreads its hood and sits up, hissing, it's nothing but bluff and pretence. It wants you to think it is much more dangerous than it really is. Frogs bloat their bodies with air to make themselves look big and scary. Snakes and lizards open their mouths wide and puff themselves up. Quite often, this is enough to frighten away the bird or other predator that is looking for food. Crocodiles and lizards also do a 'high walk', raising their bodies off the ground to look scary. It's funny to see a small gecko raising itself in this boastful posture. But it works, and another creature that is trying to invade its territory – or eat it up – will quickly retreat.

Some lizards, like geckos and skinks, can drop their tails when caught. This is a very useful trick. It directs the attention of the predator away from the head of the animal, to the tail...without which it can manage until it grows back. While the predator is puzzling over the wriggling item, the animal runs off.

Soon, another tail will grow. How is it possible to drop a tail? The muscles of the vertebrae of these animals are so loosely connected that they separate, and break off, easily. The broken part wriggles for a while because it retains its muscular activity for some time after coming off. Geckos can chuck their tails off even before they are caught! This is indeed useful. While the predator is scratching its head in wonder – or chomping on the tail – the gecko's off. However, at certain times of the year, when food is scarce, they are not so happy about dropping their tail, because that's where fat is stored.

The stout sand boa, when attacked by a mongoose or bird of prey, tucks its head under its coils and waves its tail in the air. The head and tail of this snake look very similar. The idea is to fool the predator into attacking the tail rather than the head. Sand boas often have scarred and injured tails, showing that this trick works. The spiny-tailed lizard of north-western India has a rough, horny tail which is used as a defence against snakes. Snakes are the main predators of this lizard. When it hears a snake approaching its burrow, the lizard sticks its tail out and 'attacks' the snake by shaking the tail violently. The meat of the spiny-tailed lizard is eaten by some local tribes. To catch it, they make a rustling, snaky sound with a broom outside

Sand boa

the hole and when the tail comes out, they grab it and pull out the lizard.

Others, like the ringhals of southern Africa and the American hog-nosed snake, roll over and play dead, while the trinket snake freezes in position for minutes on end, hoping to escape detection.

Ever heard a Russell's viper hiss? It sounds like a steam engine. The hissing of snakes is rather discouraging, and makes you want to be far away. Crocodiles, and even turtles, also hiss, growl, groan and moan in an effort to frighten predators. The deep, throaty growl of the king cobra and rat snake is a sound to remember. The rattlesnakes of the USA

Rattlesnake

face the enemy and shake their rattle, which is loud enough to be heard 30 metres away. People often ask why venomous snakes need to hiss, and puff, and bluff, when their venom can easily kill most of their enemies. But the snake doesn't know this! Snake venom is a type of saliva that helps it to kill and digest prey. When a snake bites a human foot that has accidentally stepped on it, its defence mechanism kicks in automatically. It doesn't know that the foot is not its prey, and that the bite will lead to a miserable time in hospital, or even death.

One of the best defences is speed. Many reptiles can move fast. A saltwater crocodile, believe it or not, can actually gallop like a horse! Some species of snakes and lizards can disappear in a flash. The poor old turtle is at a disadvantage, but its hard shell is good protection. And, come to think of it, moving very, very slowly – like the chameleon does – can be helpful too. By moving slowly, you can go unnoticed, as well as get away from the danger zone.

Another way to avoid being attacked and eaten is to hide and hope for the best. In this, camouflage is very useful. This means that the animal has the same colouring as its surroundings. A green vine snake gets lost among leaves; the mud-coloured sand boa just becomes part of the earth. Lying on the banks

Chameleon

of rivers, crocodiles look like rocks, until they are disturbed...and then – *splash*! Often, a harmless little animal mimics another more dangerous animal to fool predators. The bright red tails and fast movement of skinks are very centipede-like.

The larger reptiles, of course, have a much easier time. They have few predators and little to fear. No animal is going to mess with a large crocodile, or anaconda, or python...except humans. In their jungle homes they are master predators who can take life easy. They can cruise along the river or lie lazily in the sun without having to worry about a sudden attack. They are the lucky ones.

Snek Bilong Papua New Guinea

In 1979, we were living peacefully at the Crocodile Bank in Chennai, in a beautiful house close (too close) to the sea. It is one of those homes that visitors love, and the inhabitants find rather tiresome. Every day brings some fresh surprise: the water tank decides to start leaking, or the pump breaks down, or an army of termites starts feasting on your favourite books. The salty air creates havoc with the wiring, electrical gadgets, furniture and clothes. Once in a while monkeys drop in and eat up whatever they can find, or crack the roof by jumping up and down on it.

Crossing the living room, you may step on a gecko, or crab, or coconut beetle. In the evenings, bats fly in and out as if the place was made just for them. Sometimes a big vampire bat arrives on a hunting spree and carries off a gecko. In August–September, the carpenter ants are out in full force, and their bites are one of the most unjust experiences of life: two days of intense pain and swelling, followed by mad itching. These are things we have got used to, but guests occasionally get a little hysterical.

Anyway, the peace of this menagerie was broken when a telegram arrived asking Rom if he would like to go to Papua New Guinea (PNG) for two years to help the government there start a crocodile skin industry. Such projects involve breeding and managing crocodiles in a way that helps the native tribes make a living from the sale of crocodile skin in a legal and organized manner rather than by uncontrolled poaching.

We brought out an atlas and looked at the bird-shaped island north of Australia. Half of it, called Irian Jaya, belongs to Indonesia. The other half, the eastern slice, was an Australian colony until 1973, when it became independent.

We gathered as much information as we could about this remote, faraway land. At the time, it had some of the largest tracts of rainforest anywhere in the world. And the largest crocodiles. Tribal warfare was still happening, and so was ritualistic cannibalism. One of the most venomous snakes in the world lived there. Malaria and other mosquito-related diseases were common. Rom said a big Yes, and I said a smaller one.

A flight to Singapore, another one to Manila, and then several hours of flying over Pacific Ocean waters to a bright green jewel-like island. Our base was Port Moresby, the capital city, and we received a warm welcome from the people Rom would be working with: the staff of the Wildlife Department and the crocodile farm at Moitaka, where we would be living. The house was on stilts, and made of wood and glass. When someone came up the steps, it felt like an earthquake. We had arrived in Moresby in the middle of 'the dry', and the scrub forest around us was a tinderbox ready to burst into flame. Which it did, and a couple of times we wondered whether it was time to run for our lives. Fortunately, the fire lines, where vegetation is removed to prevent fire spreading, were a good protection and we were never in any real danger.

I have described our adventures with the crocodiles of PNG in another chapter. But this particular night we weren't after crocs, but snakes. Or rather, *snek*.

It was a dark, moonless, snaky night in Port Moresby and we were out looking for pythons. There are nine species of pythons found in Papua New Guinea. One of the most beautiful and unusual is the green tree python, which rolls itself round a tree branch to form a perfect round ball. At birth the baby green python is yellow or orange, which changes to an emerald green. Its slow, lazy movements make it easy to catch, and green pythons make good '*kai-kai*' (food) for the local people. We would often buy green pythons that were off to the market and release them in the nearby forest.

This night we were not looking for green pythons but for carpet pythons, which look a bit like our own Indian rock python. In temperament and habits they are as different from the green python as chalk from cheese. Carpet pythons enjoy biting and are easily upset. To catch one, you have to be quick on your toes, know what you're doing, and be prepared to get a good nip. They have sharp, curved teeth that can really hurt.

Rom wanted one of these fighters for a snake exhibition he was organizing for schoolchildren. So off we went, with snake bags, snake hooks and mosquito repellent. We drove to the best carpet snake habitat we knew: a mountain of biscuit tins. This pile of rusty tin was part of a war dump from the Second World War era. Fierce battles had been fought between the Allied troops and the Japanese army, and parts of Papua New Guinea had even been occupied by the Japanese for a short time.

In our wanderings through the jungles and swamps around Port Moresby, we had seen vast stretches of land strewn with Allied and Japanese army relics: bottles, tins, plates, pieces of fighter and cargo planes, bomb shackles, machine-gun barrels, even a home-made 'washing machine' using drums and pipes. And, most commonly, huge piles of biscuit tins which must have been used to transport food supplies to the forces.

The biscuit tins had almost become a part of the geography. On and between them grew lush vines, orchids and grass. After a rain, frogs would be croaking away from little pools formed in the rusty landforms. And the carpet pythons loved the tin habitat because it provided secure shelter and easy escape. No snake catcher, however expert, could follow a python here without risking a broken leg or arm.

As we approached the strange metal mountain, there was a flash of movement and colour in the grass. Rom's torch picked out the heavy body of a large snake, black and yellow. It was a D'Albertis python, named after an Italian explorer notorious for his bad behaviour towards the people of Papua New

Guinea. His namesake, however, is very different, and the shining, beautiful specimen was soon sitting peacefully in one of our snake bags.

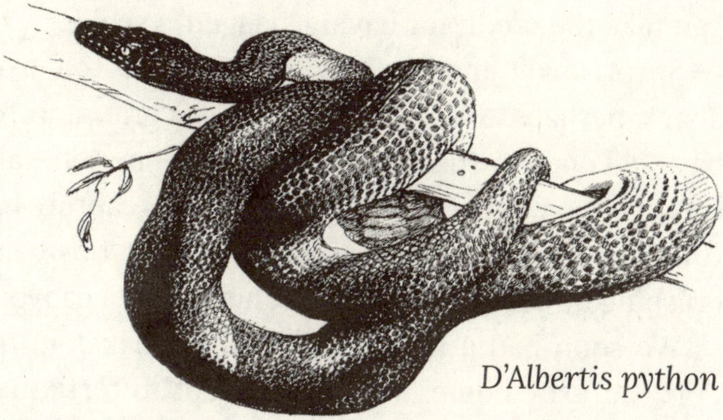

D'Albertis python

Further on, we saw what was a snake hunter's dream. On a bomb shackle sat a young carpet python, enjoying the sun-warmed metal on this cool night. And ahead of us, on the biscuit mound, were five big 'carpets', relaxing. But the torchlight had alerted them, and one shot off into a biscuit-tin canyon.

We knew there was no time to lose: the others would run off too. I stood at a safe distance and shouted instructions, and Rom leapt up and lifted one by the mid-body with his snake hook. It was a big male, about two metres long. Fortunately, its open-mouth lunges were clumsy and ineffective. It continued its angry thrashing in the bag, which I had held open to help Rom. This is not as dangerous as it sounds, because the top is hooked around a steel ring attached to a long rod. So the helper is quite safe, but can take the credit for having 'bagged' a snake!

Surprisingly, another one was still there, too taken aback, perhaps, to move. Another quick grab, another bag held open by the frightened helper – myself – and this one too was in our possession. But its capture had totally altered the landscape. The biscuit tins came crashing down, turning the mountain into a canyon.

We soon had a large collection of snakes in our Port Moresby home. Many were kept in terrariums in the garage, but some – the more decorative ones –

Carpet python

lived in our windows, which had glass slats and made perfect snake cages. One night, the big carpet python managed to muscle his way out – and disappeared. We knew he was somewhere inside the house – he couldn't have got out – but where? We climbed stools and peered into the roof beams, emptied out kitchen cupboards, squeezed ourselves under and behind beds and other furniture, but without success.

I couldn't sleep at night worrying about our baby son Nikhil: 'What if the python strangles the baby?' 'It's probably not hungry yet, it ate last week,' was the comforting answer I got. A few days later, when I was about to insist on our moving into another house, the python was spotted, cleverly concealed in a roof crevice.

However, the next case of an escaped snake was much worse. A taipan, one of the most venomous snakes in the world, was sliding across our living-room floor. Standing on the dining table, I screamed lustily, making matters even more difficult for Rom, who was pursuing the snake with his snake hook. The slippery floor, and the energy and agility of the snake, made the task tough. And the 'helper' was in no condition or mood to open a snake bag, or even get down from the table! I've often wondered what I would have done if, like the carpet python, the taipan had disappeared. I would have insisted on changing houses immediately.

I'm not a great snake handler. In fact, I'm a lousy one. When you hold a snake, it's important to be calm and relaxed, and not make any jerky, frightened movements. Well, I do, and snakes are most unhappy with me...and vice versa. Rom tried for years to train me and finally gave up. But there was one snake I could handle with confidence, and that was Pap. That was the name of our three-metre Papuan python. He never got excited, and almost seemed to like people. On being picked up, he lay in your hands like a large sack of vegetables. And everyone thought I was so brave, which naturally made me feel good. '*Missus emi no gat pret* (afraid),' the croc farm staff would say, watching me in awe and wonder. I always smiled modestly. I never mentioned that this species is the wimp of the snake world, and never ever bites.

Then, one day, Pap disappeared. Going downstairs to visit the snake cages, we saw his cage open, and empty. His heavy tracks on the driveway showed that he had taken off for the crocodile farm. Being a water python, he must have smelt the nice large ponds. If we didn't find him quickly, he would become croc food in no time. The enclosures were full of hungry saltwater crocs. We spread the message about our missing pet and the staff kept an eye out for signs of Pap. Farapo, an excellent tracker from the Chimbu tribe of the highlands, began peering closely at the ground, sometimes getting down on all fours to eyeball a faint scrape or line that was invisible to us. Feeling rather dejected, we went home.

While we were having lunch, we saw Farapo standing in our driveway, scratching his woolly head. '*Me tink snek emi kam bek*,' he said. Why on earth would an escaped *snek* come back to its prison? We went down and tried to see the track he was pointing to. But there was no need to read tracks: there, right next to his cage, was the tired Pap, breathing hard and looking apologetic. Obviously, the cage was now his home, and a strong homing instinct had brought him right back. We reinforced his cage with strong wire to prevent any further adventures.

The most famous and feared snake in this part of the world is the taipan, and Rom, of course, had been looking for one from the minute we landed in Papua New Guinea. Having been surrounded for years by snake people – people who talk of nothing but snakes – I knew quite a bit about snakes, both Indian and international. I knew that taipan venom was nerve-affecting, extremely toxic, and there was no antivenom serum for it. So, if a taipan decides to bite you, it's time to say 'bye-bye' to the world (or, if you prefer, 'farewell'). While Rom prayed for a sight of a taipan, I prayed for the opposite. It was his wish that came true, about a month after we got there. In the next 12 months, he caught seven; taipans turned out to be fairly common in the Port Moresby area.

News of the first one came from John Seba, a crocodile farm assistant. He had been walking in the scrub forest adjoining the farm and seen a large snake lying in the grass. He had backed away slowly and then run home to give us the news. We set off behind him, holding a snake hook and snake bag. I was both excited and afraid, and sweat and adrenalin flowed generously. It was the height of the Papua New Guinean summer. Located as it is in the southern hemisphere, this was not March or April as it would be in India, but November.

However, a big fat anticlimax awaited us. We got to the clearing, with John pointing wildly in the direction of the snake. But the *snek* had pushed off.

We felt foolish standing there with our bag and snake hook. However, we decided to walk a little further to a pretty stream we had visited before. It was a good turtle place, and perhaps we would see one basking on the mud bank.

We got to the stream. No turtle either. We sat on rocks for a few minutes and then prepared to walk back. Then, suddenly, there was a streak of shiny black on the opposite bank. And then, just as suddenly, Rom had long-jumped across the stream and was grabbing the tail. A flash of red on its back told me it was a taipan. And, needless to say, the snake hook was with me. Rom was taking a big chance, because taipans are alert, quick and irritable snakes.

Still, I was certainly not going to risk my own precious life to save him. The snake lunged at him, mouth open, while he did some circus moves to keep out of biting range, still hanging on to the tail. I did the only thing I could think of, which was to get across the stream and throw the snake hook at him from as far away as possible. Fortunately, he managed to grab it. There was a sense of relief all round.

Just then the snake flung itself on him. The snake hook blocked the strike. But I could see that it was getting harder and harder to keep the snake off. 'Let him go!' I yelled helplessly, knowing that that was the last thing this snake catcher. would ever do. He wanted a captive taipan, to study and photograph.

Grabbing a snake by the tail is not as easy as it sounds. Many, like the taipan, are agile, fast and intelligent. They alternate between attack and trying to defend themselves. You, the snake catcher, have to avoid being bitten as well as avoid injuring the snake. Your hold on the tail, for example, has to keep changing; otherwise, the fragile vertebrae can come apart, causing a fracture. While Rom was prancing about, John Seba and I got the bag around the wire frame. The gadget looks like a butterfly net and makes it easy to bag large, heavy snakes without injuring them.

By now our taipan was breathing hard and its lunges were getting slower and less coordinated. Scooping its head up with the snake hook and holding the tail, Rom carried the three-metre snake to where I stood holding the snake bag. He guided it towards the opening. Relieved no doubt to find a safe dark hiding place, the snake rushed in and I quickly twisted the bag shut. John Seba gave a hoot of delight and sat down to take a rest.

A few days later we had another adventure with a taipan. We were driving up to the Sogeri mountains at sunset. Suddenly, Rom screeched to a halt, so suddenly that I knew it could only be one thing: snake. He had seen a large snake crossing the road, and was off in a flash, with me following. He made a diagonal run across the road to where he thought the snake would be. But he had underestimated its speed... and I saw him shoot up in the air. He had stepped on a metre-and-a-half long taipan, barefoot! Quite a unique experience!

Termite Safari

We're on safari. The wind blows, the moon slides out from behind dark grey clouds. It disappears into another cloud-tunnel. There's excitement in the air...as there is on every safari. But it's not rhino or elephant we're after, but something just a little smaller. Termites.

After an hour of walking, I feel a bit tired but, of course, would never admit it. Dorai, our Irular companion, pokes bushes, peers at the ground, and looks up at the sky to gauge the weather, like a good hunter-gatherer. He is looking for a special kind of *puthu*, or termite mound. Finally, he finds one and whistles softly for us to come. It is a metre-high mud castle surrounded by scrub bushes. The last one, which he rejected, looked just like this one. Why did he choose this, and not that?

'Because that one wasn't ready.' He's not in a talking or explaining mood, so we shut up. I suppose what he means is that the termites were not ready to swarm, or fly out into the world.

Have you ever been in a room during a termite swarm? They crash against lights, fall into food, and generally take over the place. The next morning, their lacy wings have to be swept up. Termite swarms usually occur on cloudy nights before rain. For us city folk, it can be a nuisance. We don't particularly like insect visitors, especially in such large numbers.

However, for the people of the Irular tribe, it means snack time! Lightly roasted termites are an Irular treat. They are also very nutritious...powerful pellets of protein. There's yet another plus point for termites. They are not protected animals, and you can't go to jail for eating termites. Several other animals the Irular traditionally eat are listed in the Wildlife (Protection) Act, 1972. These include monitor lizards and several species of turtles and tortoises. However, rats and termites – two major items on their menu – are still off the list and so can be (legally) on the table!

Dorai takes a long, hard peek inside the termite mound, through one of the tiny holes. He likes what he sees. He doesn't quite lick his lips, but almost. He empties his jam-packed pockets and finds his magic seed. Lighting a small crow's nest bonfire of dry twigs, he roasts the seed over it. It is then rubbed against a stone and powdered. This seed-dust is sprinkled on the *puthu*, and Dorai sits down to wait. Waiting is a large part of the hunter-gatherer's life. But us townies are not so good at it. We look at our watches, raise eyebrows, fidget, make faces at each other.

'Bored already?' asks Dorai, and smiles.

Feeling very small, we stop acting like spoilt city creatures.

Ten minutes later, he takes another peek. 'Come and see,' he says. Squinting into the small mud canyon, I see a lot of movement. Dorai's trick has worked. The seed is supposed to smell like rain, and fool the termites into swarming, or coming out. Well, there sure is some frantic activity going on in there!

'Will they come out soon?' we ask.

'Wait,' says Dorai.

So we wait some more, trying to sit as still as him.

Yet another peep and Dorai has a big smile on his face. He takes up his crowbar and starts digging. He digs a hole near the *puthu*. In it he places an old kerosene tin he has brought along. Over the opening of the tin he makes a bridge with two sticks. And on the stick bridge he puts a small oil lamp. This has also come out of his generous pockets. He lights the lamp, and we all sit down to wait some more.

A few minutes later we hear a sound. It's a new kind of sound. A mixture of bees buzzing and faraway traffic. But it's neither. It's the termites. They've got the green signal from the boss – the queen – to leave the mound, since the weather is just right. Dorai's seed really has them fooled.

Soon, a brown trickle of insects pours out of a hole. Within seconds the *puthu* is covered with termites, all happily exploring the big wide world. There are termites in the air, termites on the bushes and ground, termites on us. But most of them make a beeline for the light...and fall into the tin. Soon the tin is full, and we empty it into a gunny sack. By the end of the safari, we have a sackful of high-protein food. Dorai and his friend pop a few live termites into their mouths. But we decide to wait until the wings are removed and they are roasted. To eat them alive you have to know what you're doing, because they can give you a good nip on the tongue!

There is a rustle in the dry grass. The termite feast is popular: a big black scorpion has invited himself and starts on the food immediately, without waiting to be asked. His table manners aren't that great. He's wolfing the food down, the way you're not supposed to. And now, here comes a huge bullfrog, almost the size of a turtle! He proves to be another greedy pig. He scoops up the termites in his mouth and leaves the wings dangling on his chin, like a false moustache. We laugh till our sides ache! Soon, he is too full to move – know the feeling? – and just sits there helplessly. After a long time, he manages to waddle away into the bushes. He looks as if he never wants to see another termite again. Know the feeling? I do. Not with termites, but with cake, ice-cream, mangoes and chocolate!

The next day Dorai brings us a small newspaper cone with roasted termites. 'Sorry, there's so little left,' he says. 'We gobbled up quite a bit last night.' At first, we are not sorry there's so little. We are not sure we can even finish what there is. But as we start munching, we wish there was. Forget peanuts and popcorn – this is the real thing!

How Scientists Can Affect the Crocodile's Love Life

The laid-back croc, he swung his tail
Slowly, from side to side,
And cruised the waters of Amarvel,
Enjoying the lazy ride.

He thought of this, he thought of that,
He pondered Death and Life;
He thought of friends, both thin and fat,
And some who had taken a wife...

Ah! There, thought the croc, is a thought
That I should really pursue –
I'm a teenager now; it's time I sought
The love of a sweetheart true.

This croc of ours was the sort of beast
Who, once a thought had struck,

Liked to act at once, or at least
Plan something that would bring him luck.

So he hauled his scales upon the bank
And waited for the ladies to come;
How lovely he looked! – all sleek and dank,
While his heart did loudly drum.

A full hour he lay there, in a debonair pose,
Making sure his tail was straight,
His head held high, well aligned with his toes,
And – oh, he could hardly wait...

Would she, wouldn't she, where *were* those girls?
This posing was really a pain;
Then suddenly, in the middle of watery swirls,
He detected a scaly mane.

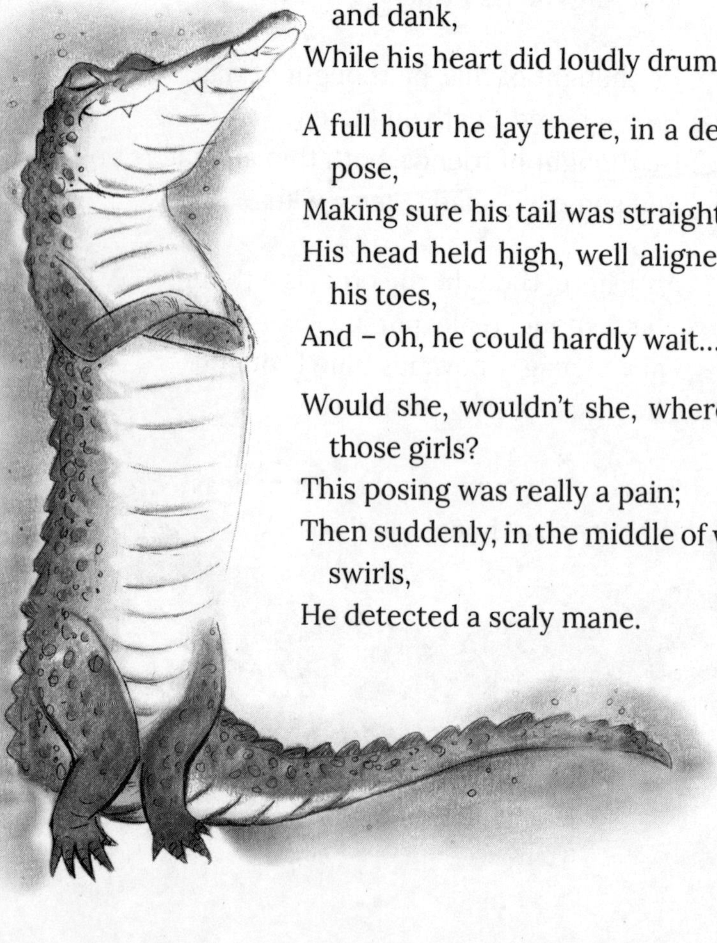

What a beautiful reptile, every scale in place,
And a sparkle in her eye;
Our croc was mesmerized by her face –
She was perfect as bandicoot pie.

She knew that the young bachelor
was watching
And did a splashy turn;
Every scale and scute on her body
tingling
With delight, from hull to stern;
Our croc he slid into the lake
And followed her with devotion –
After some moments of intense
heartache,
He began a conversation.

'Quite honestly, lady, I never did see
Anything quite so fine!
Your dorsal scutes so dazzle me
And how your occipitals shine!'

He saw she was pleased as mongoose pie
And started to plan the wedding,
When – oh, just when bliss was nigh,
Fate dealt him a horrible drubbing.

Her smile was quickly and suddenly gone
When she saw his silver tag;
'So you're one of THOSE!' she said in a tone
That made our friend's heart sag.

'Er –' he said, 'it's the survey tag –
The crocodile census, you know,
It's actually an honour, it's no great drag
And, really, it doesn't show.'

She hurried from him with a snub-nosed scowl,
Eyebrows arched in scorn;
'Let me explain!' our man did howl,
Oh, he wished he had never been born.

This un-returned love kept our friend in pain,
Nor food nor drink enhappied him;
Until finally, bliss came again
And filled him to the brim.

Another lady swam by and, with a sniff,
Said 'Oh, are you one of THOSE?
What an honour to even get a whiff
Of the wonders that science knows!'

'I've heard of this project to study our ways
By the aliens who live on land;
I can hardly avert my avid gaze
From that lovely tag on your hand!

Now quickly he struck an attractive pose
And – well, it worked out fine;
The wedding guests ate buffalo toes
And pâté of porcupine.

Ten months later, or maybe six,
Nine eggs did noisily hatch
From a nest constructed with leaves and sticks;
And as a papa, no one could match
Our ecstatic friend...

For he ferried the youngsters in his jaws
And found them crawly food,
But sometimes he scolded them because
They were just a tiny bit rude.

A Crazy Crop of Crocs

I was being hunted by hungry mosquitoes but was not allowed to hit at them. Silence was of the utmost importance. We were at a large dam in Tamil Nadu. Rom was in front of me, crouched on an embankment, holding one end of a tightly stretched net. At the other end of the net was Rajamani, an Irular who worked with Rom at the Snake Park, and was often his partner in snake and crocodile adventures.

We had come here in response to a desperate telegram from the irrigation engineer. A 2.5-metre marsh crocodile, he said, had become a nuisance to the local people. It hunted in the nearby fields, trampling crops and catching goats. We decided to go at once; more for the croc's sake than anything else. Sooner or later, people would get fed up, and kill it. This particular embankment was the croc's favourite haunt. Crocodiles are creatures of habit and often use the same place to rest and bask. This makes it easy to trap them.

Soggy from the damp ground, and carefully and silently brushing away mosquitoes, I sat as immobile as possible, ears straining. It was a very dark, moonless night. I must have dozed off several times. Around midnight I heard squishy footsteps and, startled out of a doze, backed away. A dark shape had materialized ahead of me, something between a dream and a crocodile. I prepared to get up and bolt... and just then the mugger slid into the net trap. Rom and Rajamani quickly jumped on it. It bellowed like cattle being slaughtered.

Chitra, as Rajamani named this female croc, spent the night in the irrigation office. The next morning, we unravelled her and packed her into our jeep for the ride back to Chennai. She became one of the first residents of the Madras Crocodile Bank, which we had just started.

The idea of a crocodile bank is a bit strange. Certainly not a normal kind of institution! It all started in the early 1970s, when Rom became interested in Indian crocodiles and their conservation. There were reports from all over the country about crocodile poaching, and the rapid loss of their habitat. Crocodiles live in rivers, lakes, reservoirs, dams and streams. These are also the places people like to live close to. As we know, the human population is growing fast and we have taken over more and more land that once belonged to wildlife. Because of both these reasons, crocodiles were having a hard time.

How hard? Well, it was pretty bad. Naturalists said that there were only a few hundred crocodiles left in India, quite a change from the hundreds of thousands that once inhabited our lakes and rivers. Well, so what? People didn't see this as a great problem, because reptiles – and especially crocodiles – aren't very popular animals. The fewer, the better, right? Actually, crocodiles are a very important part of the natural food chain. They are predators and scavengers, that keep our waterways clean and productive. Crocodiles are also important to the fisheries industry, because they eat the large predator-fish which, in turn, feed on the smaller fish that we consume. In lakes where the crocodile population has decreased, so has the fish catch.

Becoming interested in the plight and future of crocodiles, Rom conducted a marathon multi-state survey of the three species of Indian crocodiles: the mugger, the saltwater croc and the gharial. He and Rajamani wandered down ravines in the River Chambal, crossed the River Mahanadi in small boats, camped on the banks of lakes, rivers and dams, and travelled from state to state on motorbike, bus, lorry and train. The news they gathered was alarming. Poaching for the valuable skins, collecting of eggs for eating, and loss of habitat had put crocodiles on the brink of extinction. And so, this other kind of 'bank' was born. The plan was to breed the three species in captivity and release them back into the wild.

We started with a small group of muggers including Chitra. Soon, crocodiles were flying in thick and fast. A pair of gharial arrived from the Kukrail Gharial

Project, a group of saltwater crocodiles from the Central Leather Research Institute in Chennai. Alligators came from the United States, false gavial from Malaysia, spectacled caiman from South America. Nile crocodiles, Chinese alligators and Siamese crocodiles joined in too, and soon we had most of the world's 23 species of crocodiles.

In the early years there would be great excitement when we found a clutch of eggs in one of the enclosures. But this turned to despair as we found that the crocodiles were breeding like rabbits, and eating us out of house and home. The mugger, for example, started double-clutching. This meant that they laid two clutches of eggs every year, instead of one. The Croc Bank is the only place in the world where this has been reported. Though double-clutching is something of a compliment – it means the animals are happy and being well looked after – we got a bit anxious as the numbers multiplied! Soon we were feeding over a thousand jaws, large and small. At the same time, wild places where they could be released, were becoming difficult to find.

Rom was becoming known as a 'croc man' and was often invited to help with crocodile breeding and conservation programmes. We spent two fascinating years in Papua New Guinea while he helped the government set up a crocodile skin industry (I've written about that period in a separate chapter). When the Mozambique government decided to drain the River Zambezi's floodplain for agriculture, Rom was invited to join a study team. His job was to find out whether enough crocs remained to support a skin industry. His findings showed crocodiles could produce more income for the local people than crops.

I still have Rom's weather-beaten old croc letters and this is an extract from one of them, written from Mozambique:

> *We forged a channel in the fleshy papyrus with our machetes (knives). Frog calls rose from the two ends of the lake like a natural stereo system; closer to us, the grunting laugh of hippos foraging in the reeds. I was on Massingir Reservoir with two hefty Chengana fishermen as guides.*
>
> *When we started back across the wide lake at midnight, jagged fingers of lightning exploded from every direction. The wind picked up, gentle first, then whipping up the water until waves crashed into the side of the boat. We headed into the wind to keep from tipping over, but where was the shore? We heard the oncoming roar of the rain.*
>
> *Then another sound, closer, right under us. We'd hit a floating log, snapping the shear pin of our boat's*

propeller. Helpless, we were tossed and shoved by the wind, back across the lake. Holding on to the reeds to keep from turning over, we searched frantically for something that would replace the prop pin. Screws, pieces of wire, safety pins...these would work for a while, then snap. Eventually, we could fight the wind no longer, and found ourselves firmly stuck in a floating island of papyrus with hippos grunting and snorting all around us.

Early in the morning the wind died down, and we were able to pull loose from the papyrus stems. We got ashore using the last nail we had been able to find. It had held our only paddle together.

Thanks to crocodiles, Rom was able to visit one of the world's last truly wild places: Irian Jaya, the Indonesian province on the island of New Guinea. One of his surveys was carried out on the River Asmat, from where cannibalism has been reported. This is also where the famous anthropologist Michael Rockefeller disappeared in the late 1950s. It remains a mystery whether he was killed by one of the tribes, or drowned in a boat accident. This was then still a land of bows and arrows, tribal warfare and flamboyant headgear made of bird feathers, animal bones and turtle shells.

Here I am on the last lap of our expedition into the Asmat region. With me are the head of the WWF

[World Wildlife Fund] in Irian Jaya and two officers of the wildlife department. Our guide stayed behind, refusing to venture into the land of the 'Orang Hutan', or jungle people. It seemed like a dangerous mission, but I was sure that it was here, on the remote stretches of the Eilanden river, that we would find large numbers of crocs. Well, I guess we were a nervous party, but so far we'd only seen abandoned hunting and fishing camps of the Orang Hutan.

Then it happened. We were chugging along slowly, and there, up ahead, were four naked men walking towards the oncoming boat. All were armed with bows and arrows; one carried a carved shield. We exchanged glances: how should we react? Just then one of the men smiled and waved. We decided to stop and meet them; after all, we'd have to pass this way again on our return journey, and must be careful not to make enemies. Besides, our rubber boat would make a good target and was certainly not arrow-proof.

But it was an anxious half hour. They were uncertain about our intentions, and skittish. They muttered to each other, seemed irritated, and their arrows looked more and more dangerous as the minutes went by. Giving them chunks of black tobacco, which is popular in this area, we made a getaway.

Perhaps it had been foolish to come chugging into this hidden land. But the reward was great: hundreds of crocodiles, many of them so unused to humans that I could get on the bank and walk right up to them.

When Rom was asked to go to Bangladesh to survey the Sundarbans mangrove swamp, I was tempted to go with him, but couldn't, for some reason I forget. The disappointment turned to relief when his letters started arriving:

One reads about the man-eating tigers of the Sundarbans, but the reality of it only hit me as the survey began. An armed guard shadows me day and night, which greatly irritated me at first. But then the reminders are everywhere: accounts of the

latest attacks, warnings from the Forest Department, shorts or sarongs of victims hung on poles along the waterways to mark recent deaths. Tigers kill an estimated 100 people in the Sundarbans every year; six have died since I got here.

We've been cruising the side creeks at night in a dingy, looking for the eye-shine of saltwater crocs. By day we stumble through dense thickets of tiger fern, looking for croc nests. Tigers are constantly on our minds. Some of the biggest crocs in the world live here but are too smart to allow a close approach. On Jhinbaria Khal (creek) a five-metre salty swam lazily ahead of us for long minutes, the powerful tail swinging slowly from side to side.

That evening I took a walk inland among the spiky mangrove roots, along with my armed tiger guard. There was a sudden movement behind us and Omar spun round, cocked rifle uncomfortably close to my head. A beautiful dark cobra, hood spread and alert, stood upright watching us from the oozy chocolate mud.

And so, with each such letter, I felt more convinced that staying home had been a better idea.

Bitten!

It was March 1997, and I was peacefully sitting in the garden, reading a book, sipping lemon juice and thinking how lucky I was to have this quiet holiday when all my friends were working. Life was good, and I was going to rest and relax. My home is on the beach, next to the Crocodile Bank on the East Coast Road in Chennai. My son Nikhil works at the 'Bank', and had just gone back there after lunch.

Just then a breathless messenger arrived and shouted the words: 'Nikhil bite crocodile!' I know my sons do weird things sometimes, but they would certainly draw the line at biting crocodiles. I guessed that the words had got mixed up from excitement. When people are upset and excited, they often forget their grammar. This jumbled sentence meant that a crocodile had bitten my son.

I went numb with fright but managed to croak a question. The answer was 'Yes, it's bad.' I began to sprint towards the Crocodile Bank, wishing I was 30 years younger and could move faster. Then I slowed down: a broken leg was the last thing we needed at that moment.

I am a pessimist, and always look on the dark, rather than the bright, side. I was sure it was all over; that I had lost my son. When crocodiles bite, they like to do a good job. They take these things seriously. So I was very relieved to see him sitting up, with a huge turban around his right hand. So relieved, in fact, that I even forgot to scold, which really surprised him. But as the bandage was removed, I began to feel ill. His hand looked like a badly cooked steak, with two holes in the middle through which you could see daylight at the other end. Nikhil had lost a lot of blood; the sand around him looked like the remains of a painting competition. The pain was obviously acute, and his face was white and drained.

Frightened and panicky, I made a stupid decision. I have made a lot of mistakes in my life, but this one takes the gold. Instead of taking him to a hospital in the city, I set off for a clinic nearby. The doctor and nurses had never seen anything like this before. Doc, standing across the room, ordered the nurse to pour a bottle of hydrogen peroxide on the wound. The pain, of course, was almost unbearable. I felt like a war criminal. She then suggested anti-rabies shots, and I said that reptiles were not carriers of rabies. She wasn't pleased, and dismissed us, telling us to come back in two days.

'Doesn't it need to be stitched?' I asked.

This displeased her further. 'We will see,' she replied.

We went home, getting some strong painkillers on the way.

By next morning it was obvious I had made a grave mistake. At dawn we were at H.M. Hospital. Nikhil, by now almost crippled with pain, went in to see the doctor on duty. A surprised face surrounded by stethoscope shot out a moment later. 'What's happened?' he asked. 'The boy says he's been bitten by a *crocodile*. Please explain.'

I won't go into the details of the treatment, which was excellent. In case you ever have a croc bite problem, head straight for H.M. Nikhil's hand was embroidered with neat stitches. He was extremely lucky that the teeth had not crunched bone; there was no fracture. It was while he lay there, with a glucose drip in one arm and iced bandages on the other, that I finally got the story out of him. It is a story about the optimism of youth, Lady Luck, and the speed at which those 'sleepy' crocodiles can move.

The story begins at the saltwater crocodile enclosure. It was feeding time, and Ramesh had gone to get the feed for Jaws III, one of the biggest crocodiles in captivity in the world. The rule is that the staff should enter the enclosure in pairs, and with a pole. Jaws III is over five metres long, and saltwater crocodiles, unlike marsh crocs, don't have much fear of humans.

Looking at Jaws, Nikhil decided that he might as well go into the enclosure. Ramesh was on his way and would be there soon. Like me, my son makes mistakes; and this one could have cost him his life. He jumped in.

Jaws, being a smart croc, sensed it was lunchtime, and rushed up on the bank towards him. Nikhil leaped backwards to avoid the charge. In doing this he lost his balance, and put out his arm to steady himself.

There was a lightning snap of the big jaws and Jaws headed for the water. Nikhil had managed to stand up by then and walked along with the croc, his hand clenched between its teeth. He was buying time. Big crocs take their prey into the water, and this is what Jaws did. Nikhil knew that if he struggled, Jaws would panic and begin to 'roll'. That would be the end. Nikhil had read and observed enough about the feeding habits of crocodiles to know his only chance lay in keeping calm. This is of course not an easy matter when you are, quite literally, in the jaws of death.

The predator and prey were soon in a metre of water. The pond was two metres deep at the centre. Nikhil can't remember what he was thinking at this point. His mind seemed to have stopped working and he was only focusing on his survival. Any second now, Jaws would pull him down to drown him. Just then there was a big splash as Ramesh rushed into the water and jumped on Jaws, surprising him into opening his mouth for a split second. It was a feat of great courage, and saved Nikhil's life. Both boys leaped on to the bank, keeping the pole between themselves and the angry crocodile.

It was only when he was out of the enclosure that Nikhil realized that this entire adventure had been on display. There was a circle of stunned tourist faces along the wall. They had all kept deathly silent during the drama; lucky again, because noise would have panicked Jaws into speedy action. Later, one of the visitors asked if the whole thing had been 'real', or a show put on for visitors. He was told that the Crocodile Bank didn't sacrifice its staff for the entertainment of tourists!

Puk-Puk Bilong Papua New Guinea

In 1979, the United Nations Development Programme invited Rom to work in Papua New Guinea (PNG) for two years.

Rom began working in the Puk-Puk (crocodile) Projek Bilong Papua New Guinea and I decided to learn the fascinating national language, Pidgin. It was the only way to communicate, such as at the local market where I bought vegetables and fruit. These shared the market stalls with more interesting local foods like barbecued flying foxes and other bats, pythons and wallabies.

My first brush with Pidgin was when the house-help asked if she should make a 'bottle of *su-su*' for the baby. Now in my language '*su-su*' means piss, so I was relieved when she reached for the tin of milk powder. It is a language which doesn't waste time on unnecessary grammar and vocabulary. Helicopters are '*mix-master bilong Jesus*' and elbow is '*screw bilong arm*.' Knees, of course, are '*screw bilong leg*'. A bad fellow is a '*no-gut pella*', to eat is '*kai-kai*' and crocodile, '*puk-puk*'. Nikhil, our son, was known as '*monkey*' which means small boy, or '*pikinnini*', baby.

I got through the day very well with these few words, because our days revolved around feeding the crocodiles and feeding Nikhil. '*Yu no-gut pela, you no kai-kai*,' Rasaria would tell Nikhil. And when Rom was bitten by a crocodile at the farm next door, and one of the staff came running to tell me, '*Puk-puk kai-kai Masta*,' I said, '*Putim dispela medisin*' and sent him off with a tube of antiseptic cream.

Rom's job, helping the government with their crocodile skin project, was bringing money to some of the most remote places in Papua New Guinea, or even in the world. These were big river systems like the Sepik and Fly, which were the homes of many different tribes. Their villages were often hundreds of miles upriver, out of daily, or even monthly, reach of the outside world. They lived on fish, bird and animal meat, and a few vegetables that grew in those swampy marshes. Many of them had never even seen money. The only outside people who had been to these places, even lived in them, were the Christian

missionaries. They had tried for a hundred years to convert these 'savages' (as they referred to them) to Christianity, with limited success. Why can't we leave people alone, and let them live, and worship, as they please? What makes us force our ideas and religions on those who are different from us?

The idea behind the Puk-Puk Projek Bilong PNG was to help these river people enter the country's economy. They caught baby crocodiles in the rivers, and grew them in pens. When the puk-puks were a metre long, they were sold to the government, which would then export the skins. It was a wonderful idea because the swamp people were poor and unhealthy and, being excellent hunters, this work was ideal for them. Also, the industry would not harm the crocodile population because 80-90 per cent of baby crocodiles are eaten up by predators anyway. So their numbers would remain constant in spite of large numbers of them being caught.

Rom and the others in the Puk-Puk Projek helped the river people make rearing pens for the puk-puks, and taught them about feeding and looking after them. They told them how to identify, and treat, a sick crocodile. They shared their knowledge about the best and fastest ways to grow crocodiles cheaply. For example, different sizes should be kept separately. Otherwise, the smaller crocs are never allowed to get near the food, and they starve to death.

When a village had a bunch of crocs ready for sale, they would send a message to the Projek asking them to come and collect them. Rom and his gang would go off in a small Cessna plane, landing on a daredevil jungle airstrip that hadn't been used for months, even years. Then a 'river truck' (a sturdy flat-bottomed aluminium boat) would chug them up the river to a tiny settlement where a hundred crocs waited to be transported to Port Moresby.

Another part of their job was to study the crocodile populations on the rivers. This meant going on the rivers at night with powerful flashlights, and 'shining' the waters for eyes. Croc eyes have a reflective material called *lucidium tapetum*, which reflects directly beamed light. Suddenly, the darkness is dotted with red rubies, and it is a beautiful sight (especially when you're safely inside a big boat).

I was lucky enough to go on some of these puk-puk patrols. I travelled and stayed in villages that had seen no outsiders for generations...and no one had ever seen, or even dreamed of, an Indian. Suddenly, I became a celebrity. People would run away in fright, others would come up and touch me all over, and discuss me in detail in their '*tok ples*' or tribal language. Once you left Port Moresby, Pidgin was not much use. Then a country of 3,000,000 people, PNG has over 600 tribes, and as many languages. A totally different language is spoken from one valley to the next!

I found that being a celebrity isn't much fun. I was always being stared at and studied. One night, sleeping in a village house, I woke up with a start and...lo and behold, there were three pairs of intent eyes watching me. Spooky!

Still, the rewards were great. I visited the most beautiful places on earth. The jungles, rivers, sunsets and sunrises we saw are still painted in my mind. Some of the most fantastic, almost unbelievable, birds in the world live here, many of them endemic, which means they are found nowhere else. The nearly 40 species of birds of paradise in PNG look like they have been carefully crafted in silk, velvet and precious jewels. The colours are extraordinary: silver-green and crimson-gold, deep shining purple, bright gold, sunset orange. They have long trailing tassels on their tails, elaborate crowns and crests, and breathtaking iridescence. Iridescent colours are shining rainbow colours that change as the light changes.

The name 'birds of paradise' comes from the interesting history of these birds. It started with ladies' hats in Europe. It became fashionable, in the late 1800s, to have bird of paradise plume hats. Between 1880 and 1920, about 50,000 of these bird skins were exported every year. Because the legs – usually plain and uninteresting – were removed, the Europeans believed they were special birds which never landed, but fell from the sky, or from paradise.

I have strayed away from puk-puks. But PNG is like this; it's difficult to concentrate on one thing, so much is going on, there are so many beautiful things to see and hear.

Let me go back to one early morning in Port Moresby. We were at the airport at 6.30 a.m. to fly to Lake Murray in an old Islander plane with a young Aussie pilot. Lake Murray is at the meeting point of the rivers Fly and Strickland. An hour later we were flying over the storming Fly where it meets the ocean. Down below, in the jungles, lived people who were still to make contact with the outside world; who used stone axes, and fishing lines made of cane fibre. They wore pig-tusk ornaments in their noses and ears, bird-of-paradise feathers in their headdresses, and little else. Sometimes the women wore grass skirts, mostly for ceremonial occasions. There was no shame here about the human body; in other words, 'civilization' had not arrived.

Our little plane, with us sitting on the floor – the seats had been removed to accommodate the crocodiles it was going to take back – was circling over the crude little 'bush airstrip' on Baboa Island in Lake Murray. The control room, a bamboo hut, had to issue a strip report to enable us to land, and no one seemed to be there. After ten minutes of futile circling, we sulkily flew off and landed in Kiunga, a small mining town. We waited there until the pilot managed to contact the Baboa 'airport', then took off again.

In this roadless country with its hundreds of unusual bush airstrips, flying rules have to be strictly followed. Our pilot explained that, though our Islander was the only plane in these skies that week, he could lose his licence if he landed without clearance. When we finally landed at Baboa Island, we unloaded our bags, and 300 crocodiles in special cardboard boxes were loaded into the plane. It took off with a smart wing salute to return to Port Moresby. We were going to spend four or five days surveying the Fly for crocodiles.

That evening, as it was growing dark. I took the pride of place in the river truck, an old armchair tied down to the deck to avoid a somersault. The 35-horse-power engine chugged along slowly, with

Jerome Montague at the wheel and Rom 'shining' for croc eyes. Jerome was working for the Puk-Puk Projek too, and was both extremely lucky and extremely unlucky in being posted in this remote spot with no company except himself.

Soon, Rom started picking out eyes and I recorded the number of crocodiles seen, and their approximate size, on a data sheet. A couple of hours later, we were at the village of Kapikam. It was a moonless night and all sorts of weird bird and animal shrieks, hoots and squeals filled the air.

As the river truck bumped quietly into the mud embankment below the village, we heard a new and frightening sound. It was the sound of welcome, but we didn't know it then. It was a loud, breathless chanting, like a chorus of ghosts. The welcome song continued as we were escorted to the Kiap house, a village hut especially reserved for government officers. We were the only visitors at Kapikam in many months. The room filled with people curiously watching us as we unpacked, put up mosquito nets, and ate our dinner of biscuits and sardines. Sleeping in this kind of watched state is difficult, but I guess I was tired enough to manage pretty well.

The next morning while Jerome and Rom measured the crocodiles that were being grown for the Projek, I walked around the village with my procession of fans. I saw a lady suckling a baby pig at her breast, a common sight in PNG. All the women wore grass skirts and the men had a shell band around the waist. Most of them were covered with grille, a fungal skin disease that looks like a delicate tattoo of pin-pricks. Some women were pounding sago, the staple diet here. A group of men carved deadly looking arrows with fine fish-bone barbs on them. It was here that we were presented with a sword-like weapon with shark teeth on both sides. We wondered whether it was for hunting, or warfare.

At villages like Kapikam, I felt transported into another world. Here, time stood still and life was simple, peaceful and uncomplicated. No, not always peaceful; because tribal warfare was a part of everyday life in PNG. I experienced this at close quarters in the highlands, when we arrived at a scene just after a 'payback' fight because one tribe had killed pigs belonging to another.

Towards us however, there was always friendliness and hospitality. As soon as we arrived at a village, however remote and far away, a room would be offered for the night, and food. It wasn't always the kind of food we were used to: roasted maggots, grilled python and other such jungle goodies were enthusiastically presented to guests as special treats. I quickly learned to pat my tummy in a 'I'm too full right now' gesture.

Lizards Are Wizards

Lizards are a fascinating group of animals. A good example is the chameleon, which is both a clown and a monster in appearance. It changes colour like a kaleidoscope, depending on its emotions and feelings at the time. Special cells in the lizard's skin allow it to do this. Chameleons have a prehensile tail, like a monkey's, which curls tightly around branches to give it balance and support, and keep it from falling. The head is encased in a sort of motorcycle helmet. The round eyes rotate independently of each other, looking for insect prey in every direction. When a grasshopper or other tasty morsel is sighted, both eyes focus on it, like a pair of small binoculars. A long tongue – like stretched bubblegum – shoots out and 'stabs' the prey. Its sticky tip is a great capturing machine.

By the way, chameleons are supposed to be insectivores (insect eaters) but we've seen one eating a frog. Indian natural history is full of gaps; we still know so little about even the common animals that live around us. Of the 7,000 species of lizards in the world, about 270 live in India, in habitats ranging from high-elevation forests to deserts. Lizards do amazing things. The basilisk of South America runs on water, which is why it's called the 'Jesus Christ Lizard'. An Indian lizard, the draco, actually flies. It uses its leathery wings, called patagia, to glide down from the tall rainforest trees, which are its home. Some lizards run on their hind legs, like little kangaroos. Certain gecko species are all-female; the females have both male and female reproductive organs and can produce fertile eggs!

The lizard we see most often is the garden lizard, or bloodsucker as it is unfairly called. This name may have come from the blood-red crest on the neck, which the male develops during the breeding season. Garden lizards have a fascinating lifestyle, about which we still know very little. They have a strange communication system and often bow to each other for long periods. At other times, they nod their heads from side to side, or do little push-ups.

It is of course exciting to see tigers and lions and elephants, but observing the most common birds and animals can also be fascinating. I was once walking down a road and came upon a female garden lizard laying her eggs. I decided to be late for my appointment and watch this interesting spectacle. She had dug a little hole about ten centimetres deep in the dry earth; this must have taken a lot of time and energy. She laid twelve eggs, which took about half an hour. Then she replaced the dug earth over the eggs with her hind legs...and I thought the show was over. But no, the best part was still to come. She suddenly lowered her head and, using it like a hammer, began to pack down the earth. She must have ended up with a bad headache, I'm sure.

Garden lizards belong to a group called agamids, one of eight families of Indian lizards. The smallest

Draco

Desert lizard

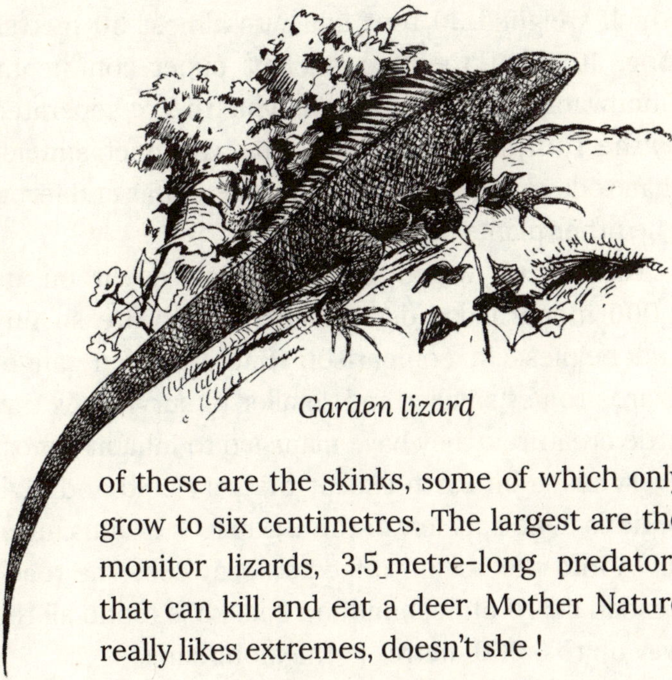

Garden lizard

of these are the skinks, some of which only grow to six centimetres. The largest are the monitor lizards, 3.5 metre-long predators that can kill and eat a deer. Mother Nature really likes extremes, doesn't she !

What exactly is a lizard? The word comes from the Latin word *lacerta*. Lizards are reptiles with long bodies that lay eggs; they have scales and, usually, legs. The lucky ones have four, but some have only two, or none. Lizards arrived on earth about 200 million years ago, during the Triassic Age. The leading lizard of that period was the impressive Diplodocus, which weighed 30 tons and was almost 30 metres long. It ruled the two ancient super-continents, Gondwanaland and Laurasia, which were separated by the Tethys Sea. The landscape was much simpler than today's rich vegetation...mostly palms and ferns. The other plants had yet to evolve.

Diplodocus would certainly look down on its 3,000 modern-day descendants, which are so tiny and helpless in comparison. But evolution taught lizards to get smaller and smaller to survive. As tiny little creatures, they have managed to inhabit almost every place on earth except the very cold and high regions. One species, in the Galapagos Islands, even dives into the ocean to feed on seaweed. The toad-headed lizard of Kashmir and Ladakh is found all the way up to 6,000 metres in the mountains.

The lizard that comes closest to the 'Dip' is the monitor lizard. The first monitors to walk the earth

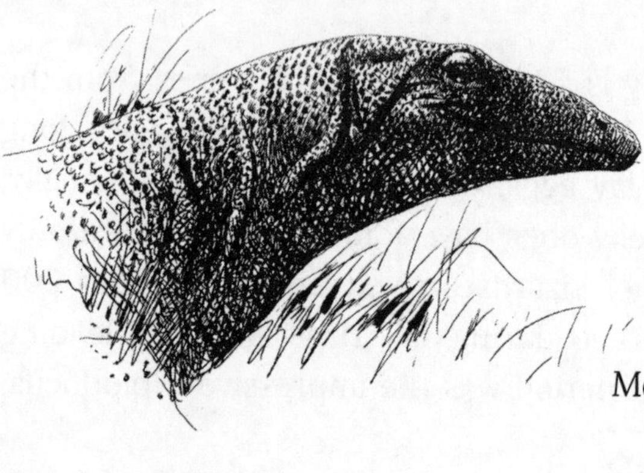

Monitor lizard

were 10 metres long. Today the largest is the Komodo dragon of Indonesia, which grows to three metres and weighs over 100 kg. Scientists discovered the Komodo only in 1912! Before that, they would simply laugh at traders' stories about the giant reptile that could kill deer, pig and even cattle. In India we have four species from this family, the largest of which is the water monitor that also grows to about three metres.

Monitors are carnivores (meat eaters) and feed on insects, rats, frogs, fish, birds, snakes...anything that moves...alive, dead or even very dead. We have seen monitors feeding on old and stinking cattle carcasses. In Sri Lanka, they hang around garbage dumps like stray dogs. Not all lizards are carnivores, however; several, like the Himalayan rock lizard, are vegetarian. The bright green day gecko of the Andaman Islands licks nectar from coconut flowers. Vegetarian lizards may have special bacteria in their intestines that help them digest plant tissues, just like cows, turtles and other animals do.

To get back to the more common lizards, we all know the good old *chhipkali* (*palli* in south India), which races up and down our walls and ceilings. There are over 850 species of geckos worldwide. Geckos have special toes with discs that serve as suction pads; with these, they can 'stick' to the wall.

Sometimes though there is a mechanical fault and a gecko lands on your head or lap, not a very pleasant experience for many.

You might have seen a gecko licking its eyes with its long tongue. Unlike most lizards, geckos have no eyelids. It is the job of the tongue, therefore, to keep the eye cover clean.

The poor harmless gecko is not very popular in India as some people believe they are poisonous. This is not true. Sometimes there are stories in the newspapers about people getting sick from eating food in which a gecko had fallen. No; they got sick because the food was rotten, or adulterated. All Indian lizards are absolutely harmless; the world's only poisonous lizards are the Hila monster and the bearded lizard of the United States and Mexico.

Not all geckos are as small as the ones in our homes. The *tokay* or *tuk-too* of north-east India is a 25-centimetre fighter with a loud call and a lot of courage. Tokays will battle snakes, even large rat snakes. When attacked by a predator, it opens its mouth wide, which is quite a scary sight. A *tuk-too* bite can be pretty painful, so a wise predator would quickly change its mind and go looking for other prey.

Skinks, those glossy, fast, snaky-looking lizards, are common residents of our parks and gardens, and

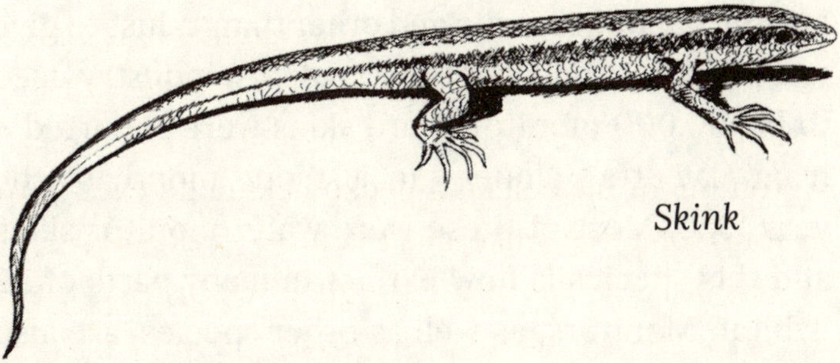

Skink

there are about a thousand species in the world. Many skinks protect their eggs and young. Although lizards generally lay eggs, the streaked skink of Assam and some other species bear living young. The nesting habits of lizards show these animals to be smart and practical. The female Bengal monitor lizard, for example, lays her eggs in a termite mound. Termites are vicious and defensive about their mounds so of course the eggs get good protection from predators! The female monitor manages to slip in, lay her eggs and get out without being attacked by the insects. The temperature and humidity of the mound is also ideal for the incubation of eggs. Eight or nine months later the baby monitors hatch and dig their way out into the world.

Unfortunately for lizards, they are good-looking and have beautiful skins. Several species have become rare because their skins were used for making handbags, belts and other things. Just to give you an idea of how big the lizard skin industry used to be, 60,000 monitor lizard skins were exported – from Calcutta* alone – in just one month of the year 1930. Most of these were water monitor skins and this species is now extinct in many parts of its habitat. Monitors, as well as other species, are also killed for their meat. In the arid desert regions of north-west India, the sanda, or spiny-tailed lizard, continues to be killed for its meat, which is supposed to have medicinal properties.

The government has protected several species of lizards in the Wildlife Act. This Act makes it illegal to keep or kill lizards. However, there are always people willing to break the rules, and poachers still go after protected animals because of the money they bring in for their skin and meat. Other species of lizards are becoming rare because the forests they live in are being cut down. As each animal – whether a lizard or mammal or something else – becomes rarer, or extinct, the balance of nature is upset even further. Unless people realize the importance of protecting them, our own lives are in danger. Because the smallest gap in the chain of living things causes big

Now Kolkata

problems in the environment. For example, in areas where snakes and lizards have become rare, the rat population is booming. And, as you know, rats eat up our food. While people starve, rats get fatter and

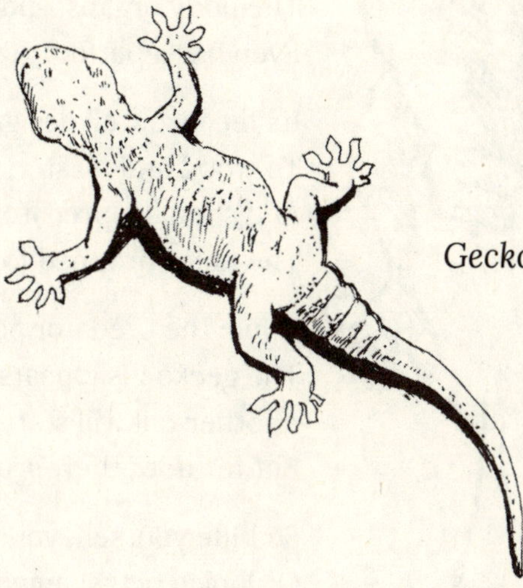

Gecko

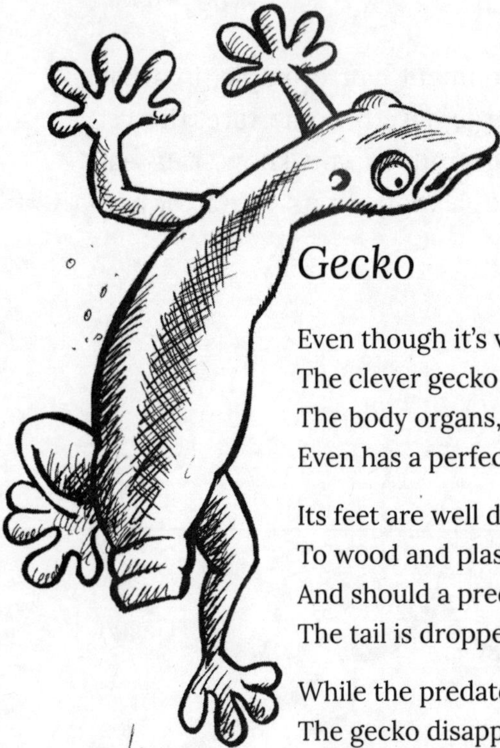

Gecko

Even though it's very small,
The clever gecko possesses all
The body organs, and this lizard
Even has a perfect gizzard.

Its feet are well designed, and stick
To wood and plaster, stone and brick;
And should a predator grab it for lunch,
The tail is dropped for it to munch.

While the predator ponders this mystery,
The gecko disappears, uneaten and frisky.
Another tail will start to grow,
But for now, there's just a stub to show.

So hide yourself, you tailless beast,
Or look a bit ashamed, at least!
Please...this tail manoeuvre don't repeat
It makes you look so incomplete!

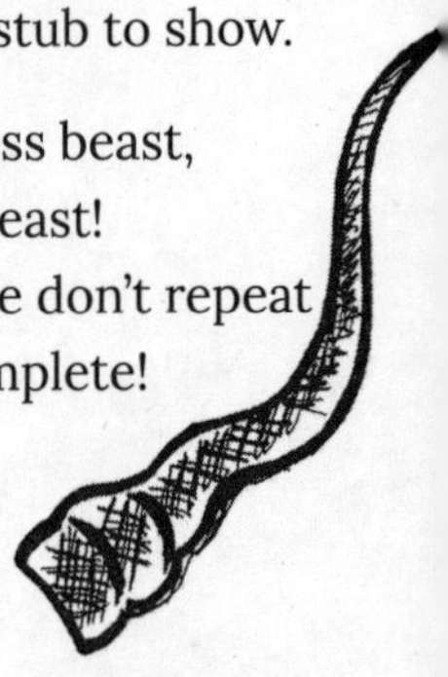

Turtles and Tortoises

Nowadays we hear much more about sea turtles than about freshwater turtles and tortoises. Sea turtles get a lot of attention in the media because: they are large and easy to spot, they nest on our beaches, and many naturalists are working to protect them and their nesting sites. But freshwater turtles and tortoises are also a very interesting group of reptiles. Scientists call them chelonians, pronounced *cheh-LOW-nians*. Indian chelonians belong to three distinct groups: the soft-shell turtles, the hard-shells, and the tortoises. They come in a range of shapes and sizes, and add up to 29 species.

The differences between turtles and tortoises are not obvious. The general rule is that turtles live in water while tortoises are terrestrial (land dwelling). But quite often, animals don't follow these rules and there are some exceptions to this one as well. For example, the cane 'turtle' is largely terrestrial, and some tortoises really love water!

One of the best-known tortoises is the star tortoise. You have probably seen a picture of this lovely animal: the shell has an eye-catching brown and yellow design. Every once in a while, there is an article in the media about airport officials finding thousands of star tortoises being shipped off to foreign countries to be sold as pets. This is illegal; but since people pay big money for unusual pets, the exotic-pet business is hard to control.

Not all chelonians are so colourful. Some turtles, like the Indian black pond turtle, are drab and dull, and may as well be rocks or boulders. As in birds, the males of many species are more attractive than the females. The male crowned river turtle is a handsome creature, with multicoloured stripes on the neck and face during the breeding season.

How big are turtles and tortoises? Well, the male Brahminy river turtles are as small as an adult human palm, and daintily nibble on water plants, while the Ganges soft-shells are large enough to catch and kill a young sambar deer! Freshwater turtles and tortoises are found in an interesting variety of habitats: from scrub forest in the dry plains to – the ocean! Yes, the sea-going batagur turtle

Brahminy turtle

Flap-shell

spends time in the marine lagoons and backwaters of West Bengal. And way up in the foothills of the Himalayas lives the elongated tortoise. But most of the Indian species live in and around lakes, rivers and ponds on the plains. The most common are the Indian black pond turtle and the flap-shell. They are found throughout the Indian subcontinent. Others have more restricted ranges; for example, the cane turtle lives only in parts of the Western Ghats in southern India.

It was the cane turtle that took me on an exciting visit to a rainforest in Kerala. I was working at the Snake Park then, and one of our colleagues, the 'turtle-girl' J. Vijaya, had rediscovered this species, which was thought to be extinct. It was a great discovery and Vijaya invited me to visit her and the rare turtle. After a long, exhausting walk through the forest, I came upon Vijaya's 'home', a small cave that had earlier been used by animals. She had had to do a thorough house-cleaning before moving in, sweeping out the remains of old panther kills and bear droppings. Fortunately, we only had a small scorpion for company, and at my insistence Vijaya carried it gently outside and encouraged it to run away and return only after I left!

We were constantly on the lookout for elephants; their signs and sounds were everywhere and since we were busy looking at the forest floor for turtle signs, it would have been easy to crash into a jumbo. We roamed the forest with hunters of the Kadar tribe, who used to catch and eat cane turtles before Vijaya's arrival. We were lucky to see a couple of these rare animals, nibbling on mushrooms growing not far from the cave. This was paradise on earth: just below the thick forest surrounding us, ran a cold, clear stream where we bathed and washed our clothes. The Kadar women sat on the rocks, crushing and grinding tree bark to make their soap, and snail shells for lime to chew. One afternoon we watched a Kadar honey collector climb a home-made cane ladder to a 30-metre-high treetop to reach a large beehive.

The soft-shell turtles lay almost perfectly round eggs, while the hard-shells lay elongate (long and oval) ones. Most turtles lay eggs that are hard and brittle. Some have pliant and soft eggs. Egg clutches number from one to fifty, depending on the species. The incubation period, or hatching time, also differs according to the temperature and other factors. It could take a baby turtle anything from a few weeks to a few months to hatch. In most species the laying and incubation of eggs is almost computer programmed so that the little turtles arrive with the rains. For

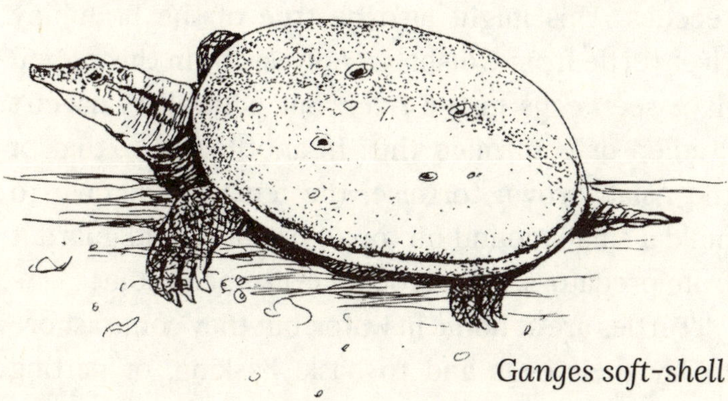

Ganges soft-shell

young animals – reptiles, mammals or birds – rain means food. Insects, tender plant shoots and baby frogs are plentiful and they can grow fast.

One interesting 'trick' discovered in the Ganges soft-shell is that the female can continue to produce hatchlings for 15 years without the presence of a male! She does this by storing male sperm in her body and using it gradually over the years.

There may be other fascinating turtle stories waiting to be discovered. Despite the large number of turtle species in our country, and their importance in our ecology and economy, not much is known about them. For example, the long-necked turtle from Australia is known to deposit its eggs underwater. What a smart and safe place, away from many egg-loving predators! The eggs start to develop about twelve weeks later, when the water recedes. This might also be true of the Brahminy river turtle from Odisha, as Adivasis from this region have seen eggs in the river. But naturalists haven't studied or confirmed this. In another case, that of the Asian brown tortoise, the female is known to build a small mound on top of her nest, and guard it from predators. Very crocodile-like behaviour!

Turtles are at home in water, but they come ashore to lay their eggs and to bask. Basking, or getting warm, is an important activity for all cold-blooded animals. When there is too much disturbance and human activity in their habitats, they keep jumping into the water from fear and don't get enough basking time. This lowers their body temperature, and they could get sick and even die. This condition is typical in captive turtles, where there is not enough warmth in the cage or aquarium. Herpetologists (scientists who study reptiles) feel that basking also helps in digestion, parasite-control and making vitamin D. In times of drought, turtles have to walk long distances on land to seek water. This is tough for an aquatic creature. Turtles are most vulnerable at these times and can be easily killed. Many thousands of turtles perish every year when water dries up and the rains come late, or fail.

At first glance, turtles appear to have been cheated with regard to defending themselves compared to other reptiles. They don't have venom, like many snakes do. Nor do they have tails to lash out with like the monitor lizards, or deadly teeth like the crocodiles (indeed, turtles only have a serrated horny beak, also known as the 'rhamphotheca'). But wait, it's not as bad as it sounds. The hard-shells, of course, have an armour that even the most powerful predator jaws can't penetrate. They duck inside their shell when disturbed. This is a useful defence mechanism that has saved many a turtle from many a predator. And like all good weaponry, this armour is strong, and a product of millions of years of evolution. The box turtles of North America and South-East Asia can support 200 times their own weight!

The soft-shells aren't so lucky, and they have to use other tricks and techniques to escape predators. The Indian black pond turtle is accurately named '*pee-aamai*' in Tamil, because when you pick it up, it lives up to its name... And when it comes to the larger soft-shells, they can give you a serious nip, and even remove a bite-sized chunk of you in a flash. There are stories of people having fingers, toes and other body parts bitten off. Soft-shells are spirited warriors that claw, scratch and bite...and even whack with their heads! The huge narrow-headed soft-shell is reported to attack small boats. This may be a slight exaggeration, but it gives us an idea of the size and spirit of the animal. Young chelonians are especially at risk, of course, and some have bright 'eye' markings on the shell to frighten away predators (like those usually found on butterflies and moths). These disappear as the turtle grows.

Another interesting fact about the narrow-headed soft-shell is the way it catches its food, which is mainly live fish. Now, it's not an easy matter for a turtle to catch fish; the prey is so much faster than the predator. This soft-shell solves the problem by burying itself in the river bottom, with just the head sticking out. Lying very still, it waits patiently for a fish to swim past and then...the long neck shoots out. Snap, gulp. Large soft-shells can also pull ducks underwater. They use the same technique for large frogs and even baby crocodiles. They are good scavengers as well, and a cattle carcass may have a group of large soft-shells pulling and tugging at the rotting meat. Many turtles, such as the tent turtle, start out as carnivores - meat eaters - and later switch over to a vegetarian diet. The protein-rich food in the early stages helps the turtle grow and get strong. Some species are also cannibalistic - eating their own kind - and happily gobble up any babies that may be around.

People often wonder about the longevity of turtles and tortoises. That means their lifespan, or how long they live. We still know very little about this, but the general rule appears to be that larger species live for longer periods of time. A giant tortoise from the

Seychelles in the Indian Ocean lived for 152 years! That is a pretty long time, but turtles have been on earth for much, much longer, of course... Fossil findings show they were around when the dinosaurs were, 200 million years ago. They have survived, and adapted to, many dramatic changes including shifts in vegetation and climate, and the arrival of the mammals. Little fossil study has been done in India. One famous fossil, the Siwalik tortoise, had a shell almost two metres long! As long as a bathtub. There may be many more prehistoric monster turtles waiting to be found. Who knows? This is the wonderful thing about Indian animals and birds; so much is yet to be done. Every naturalist in our country is a lucky pioneer.

Like sea turtles, many species of chelonians are becoming rare. Their habitat is being destroyed by humans; our continuing bad habits of clearing forests, building dams, and messing up the environment, are no good for turtles. The forest dwellers suffer, and die, because cutting down trees changes the temperature of the forest floor. It gets too hot for them to survive. Herpetologists feel that many Indian species may become extinct very soon. How sad that would be.

In fact, it would be much more than just sad: it may change our lives too. Chelonians play a big part in keeping our waterways – our rivers, lakes and ponds –

clean. They eat rotting meat such as the carcasses of animals, and thus prevent disease and infection. Many dig tunnels during the drought seasons, which are also used by frogs, toads and other animals that need a cooler temperature to survive.

The pet and meat trade is another challenge that chelonians face. Turtle meat is a delicacy in many parts of our country and some states, such as West Bengal, Odisha and Uttar Pradesh, used to have large turtle markets, which included common species like the flap-shell as well as rarities like the crowned river turtle and the spotted pond turtle. Their meat and organs were exported to South-East Asian countries where people believe they have medicinal value. Although these markets have been banned, some exploitation and smuggling continues, and is a challenge for the authorities.

What is the answer to this problem? Some countries allow limited trade, or commercial farming for meat. But then how do we control that? It would just create a bigger and bigger market, and illegal killing and capture would also grow.

We can only hope that our chelonians, especially the rare species, will not disappear altogether. After all, chelonians are not just important to our environment, they are also a rich part of our culture and religion. The tortoise Kurma is an incarnation of the god Vishnu. It was Kurma who helped the gods churn the Ocean of Milk; and Kurma is also Vishnu's vehicle. The *vahana* of the river goddess Yamuna is the Ganges soft-shell turtle. Turtles and tortoises are worshipped in temples across the country. We visited one such shrine in Tripura, where devotees fed large soft-shells with pieces of meat and fish spiked on long sticks.

Like many other animals in our country, chelonians are both worshipped and exploited. It is time we listened to the herpetologists and scientists, and left them undisturbed to lead their quiet, fascinating lives in the forests and waterways of our country.

What Happened to the Reptiles?

You may not believe this story. But I can tell you it is true, because I have been to Pambupatti, the village of the snakes.

Pambupatti is in a jungle so thick, so dark, that you would think no one could ever walk through it. Fallen trees and branches block the path. Vines and creepers with cruel, hooked thorns spring at you, scratching your arms and legs. A few minutes of ducking and dodging, and you are ready to turn back. Enough! Let the lizards and the snakes and the eagles keep their jungle. We humans have better places to go to!

However, if you decide to stay, you find out that Pambupatti is on the edge of the jungle. It is on a cliff, and the vast forest stretches below like a mossy green carpet. Eagles float on the air above, peering between the treetops for a rat or a snake to pounce on. Sometimes there is an ear-splitting crash, as if a giant has put his foot on a tree and crushed it. Elephants, maybe. Or bison.

But no one in Pambupatti is the least frightened of these sounds.

There are many kinds of people in the village – dark, fair, tall, short. They speak many languages. Some eat meat, some don't. Some pray in a small temple at the edge of the forest. Others pray in a mosque, some miles away. Some worship one god, others many. But they all live so happily together!

Yet, Pambupatti was not always like this. People used to fight, and quarrel, and even kill, because some

were different from the others. If a person spoke a different language, they were kicked out. If someone prayed to a different god, they were also thrown out, or even attacked with sticks and stones! Those were bad times...and it was the reptiles who taught them a lesson. So the story goes.

At that time there were no tigers or panthers or elephants in the Pambupatti forest. There were only reptiles. Many, many kinds of reptiles.

Now, you know what reptiles are. Snakes, crocodiles, turtles, lizards. And you know that a reptile has scales on its body and it lays eggs. Well, most do anyway. There are always exceptions in nature. For instance, we can't even say that birds are creatures that fly! Because some, like the...well, never mind.

Every month, the reptiles of Pambupatti had a big meeting. Everyone came – the excited, pretty snakes, the slow, thoughtful tortoises, the clever, quick lizards, the grumpy crocodiles, a bit upset because they were out of water.

The president of these meetings was Makara, the biggest crocodile of the forest. People say he was 8 metres long, though we can't really be sure of that. But we know that the animals thought he was very important. When someone is strong and powerful, you know, it is difficult not to go along with what he says or does.

Now, one day, a strange thing happened. It was a week before one of the monthly meetings. Makara sent a letter to the tortoises, asking them not to come to the meeting. Ahisthay, the big old star tortoise with black and yellow pictures on his shell, was very angry.

'What does this mean!' he shouted. 'How dare they!' But not one of the tortoises had the courage to attend the meeting – they were so few, the others so many!

The giant Makara polished his teeth till they sparkled, using the red flowers of the tree by the river. Everyone was waiting for him at the meeting place. He walked up to the stage, trying not to grin too much. But he was rather happy with himself, so it was difficult not to.

'Brothers and sisters,' he began. All the reptiles, even the beautiful king cobras, stopped talking. Makara continued his speech, 'I have decided that we

don't need the tortoises! I have told them not to come today. Brothers and sisters, tell me why we don't like the tortoises?'

The reptiles looked this way and that. They felt very uncomfortable. The snakes hissed anxiously, the lizards wriggled their tails, the crocodiles opened their jaws even wider.

'But...' said one little lizard.

'No BUTs!' shouted Makara. There was silence.

'I think...' said a baby crocodile.

'No I THINKs!' screamed Makara, so loudly that the fruit in the tree above him rained down.

After that, no one had the courage to speak.

Makara cleared his throat and showed a few more teeth.

'Well,' he said, 'I will tell you why we don't like the tortoises.

They are so slow! So stupid! They even carry their houses on their backs – whoever heard of such a stupid thing? Now you lizards, you live in trees. Would you ever carry a TREE on your back?

Would you?'

Small, frightened voices answered, 'No, we wouldn't. But...'

'NO BUTs! Now listen. I have told the tortoises that they will have to move out of Pambupatti. When they

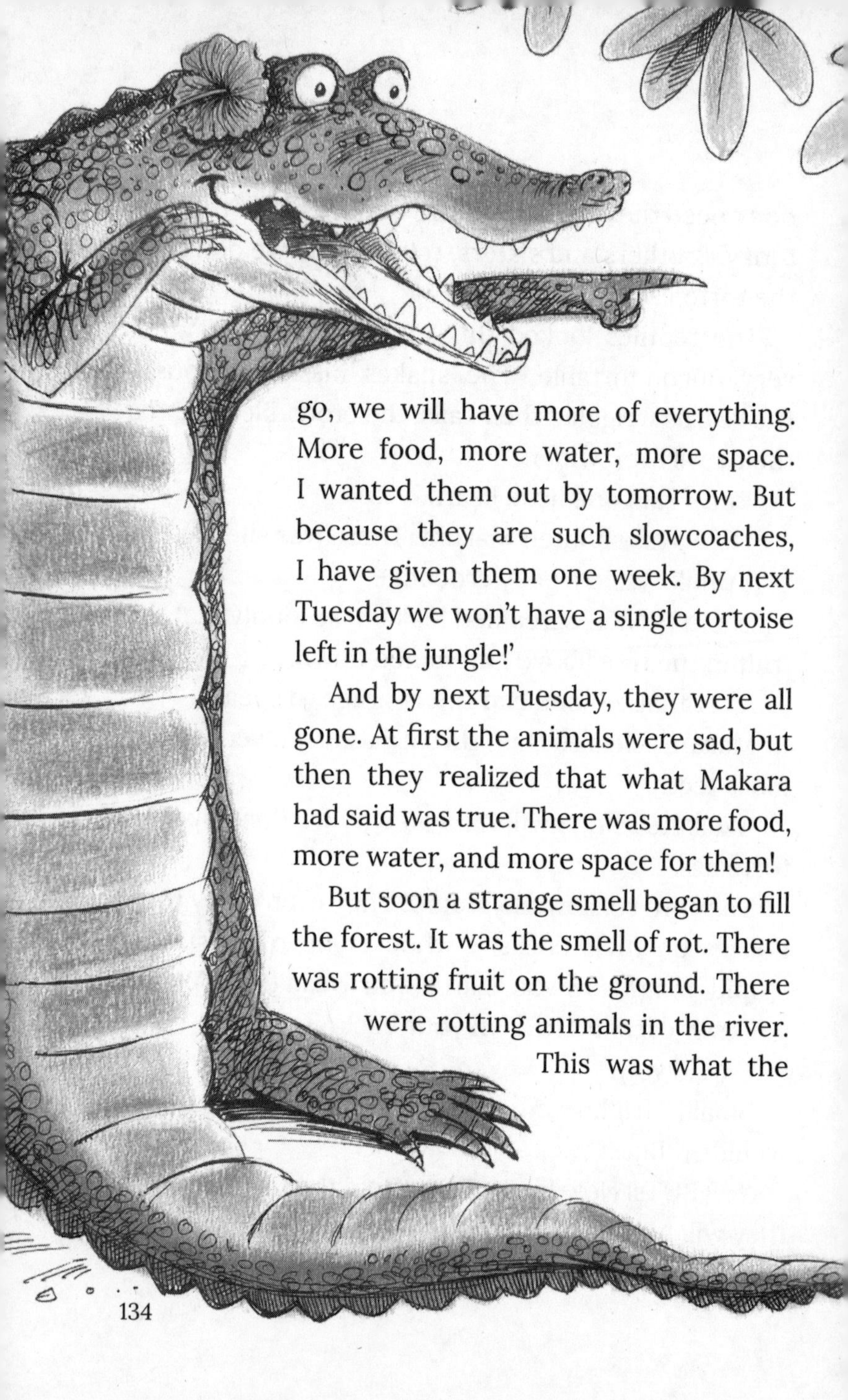

go, we will have more of everything. More food, more water, more space. I wanted them out by tomorrow. But because they are such slowcoaches, I have given them one week. By next Tuesday we won't have a single tortoise left in the jungle!'

And by next Tuesday, they were all gone. At first the animals were sad, but then they realized that what Makara had said was true. There was more food, more water, and more space for them!

But soon a strange smell began to fill the forest. It was the smell of rot. There was rotting fruit on the ground. There were rotting animals in the river. This was what the tortoises used to eat. And even Makara had to go about holding his nose with his great big claws.

A month passed by...and then the same thing happened all over again. But this time, it was the snakes. Makara sent them a message. They were to leave the forest, and since they could move fast, they had to go in a day!

Naga, the head of the snakes, pleaded for more time, but Makara would not give in. At the meeting he silenced the others – the lizards and the crocodiles – with even louder shouts and threats. 'Snakes are slimy,' he said, 'and long, and they make funny noises. Who wants such weird creatures around?' Again, no one dared to disagree with Makara and so the snakes left.

For a while the animals of the forest were happy because they had been a little afraid of the snakes. You never knew when one of them might lose his temper and spit some venom at you! And it took only a little venom to kill you, after all.

A few weeks passed and the animals of the forest looked tired and fed up. Life was getting very difficult. THE RATS! Now that there were no snakes to eat them, the rats had taken over the forest. And they were having a wonderful time. They were everywhere – on the trees, in

the grass, in the bushes, on the ground. They ate up the eggs of the lizards and crocodiles: there would be no babies that year. Even Makara's own nest of eggs had been chewed up.

Then Makara had a great idea. He called a meeting of the crocodiles and said, 'Wouldn't it be wonderful if we – the crocodiles – could have the WHOLE jungle to ourselves? No one but us? These lizards, now, just look at them! They have the strangest habits, and some of them even change colour! How can we trust someone who is green one minute, yellow the next? And they change colour, so often it's difficult to even spot them. Let's get rid of them.'

By now the crocodiles were really scared of Makara... they had got into the habit of believing everything he said. So they clapped and shouted, 'Hurray, Hurray!'

Makara was pleased. The lizards left the forest, some of them carrying their eggs and babies on their backs.

But now, when life should have been wonderful for the crocodiles of Pambupatti, all kinds of awful things began to happen. It was as if a madman had come to the forest, and was turning everything upside down. To begin with, the rats grew bolder by the day. They became so fearless that they jumped and turned somersaults on the crocodiles' backs! And there were too many frogs – they seemed to be growing larger, and there was no one to eat them but the crocodiles. These huge frogs began to eat the baby crocodiles! And the insects! Now that the lizards were gone, there were millions of them, growing bigger and nastier by the day.

It was a terrible time for the crocodiles. They couldn't understand what had happened to their happy forest home. Until one day, a squeaky little voice piped up at one of their meetings: 'We know why the forest has gone crazy, don't we?'

Suddenly everyone was silent. They looked at Makara fearfully, but to their surprise he looked nervous. He shook a pesky rat off his tail and asked the small crocodile, 'Why, little fellow?'

'It all began with the tort...'

'Okay, okay,' said Makara. 'There's no need to talk so much.' Makara didn't want to admit he was wrong, but it didn't matter. All the crocodiles knew now that he was not all that strong or powerful. Or always right. They sent urgent messages all over the place – for the tortoises, snakes and lizards to come back to Pambupatti. And what a great day it was when these creatures came back, family after family, with their little ones on their backs or straggling behind, shouting for their parents to wait for them!

In two months, the forest was back to normal. The rats disappeared, and the insects, and the smell – and the world finally seemed normal again.

But often people won't listen to this story, or they laugh and say it isn't true. Don't let that stop you from telling the story again and again, to more and more people.

Because one day they may realize that each of us has an important place in this strange, funny world of ours.

Zai Whitaker

The Turtle's Burden

Turtles are funny, it's hard to tell
What they do inside their shell.
I guess they do nothing but try to hide,
But it must be so hot and dark inside!

Now if they had a little tube light,
It would improve their spooky plight –
Because if a turtle's really scared of
  the dark,
Life must be tough, and hardly a lark.

As it is, this turtle life
Is a burden, and full of strife;
Carrying your house wherever
  you roam...
You never go out, you're always at home!

Sea Turtles' Secrets

It was a strange and wonderful sight. Like something from a science-fiction movie. Sitting on the beach on that cold December evening, covered with sea spray, we even forgot to breathe for a moment. Because there, ahead of us, was a glowing object emerging from the waves. Oval in shape, and about a metre long.

It was exactly what we were looking for: a female olive ridley sea turtle, coming ashore to lay her eggs. The glow was from the phosphorous that fills the sea and sand at certain times of the year. While walking along the beach earlier that night, our footsteps had thrown up sprays of gleaming sand, and the waves had been silver and gold. Just like fairyland. We had walked for three hours, then sat down on the dry sand to rest before turning homewards. The glowing ocean visitor had chosen her time of arrival well! A minute later, and we would have missed her.

We were on a 'turtle walk'. This doesn't mean walking like a turtle, but a beach walk during the sea turtle nesting season. In Chennai, where I live, the olive ridleys lay their eggs from November to February. They usually nest between midnight and early morning, which is a bit inconvenient for us humans. Ridleys are one of the five species of sea turtles that nest on the Indian coast, and all are endangered. Their nesting places are disappearing because of construction and human disturbance. Their eggs are eaten by human and animal predators. These include stray dogs, lizards, jackals, crabs, mongoose, rats and birds. What chance do they have! Ninety per cent of the eggs are destroyed in this way.

The few baby turtles that do manage to hatch, have a tough life ahead of them. On hatching, they may immediately get eaten up by crabs or birds. If they do make it to the sea, there are all kinds of fish and other animals (and birds) that love hatchling sea

turtles. Scientists say that only one – ONE! – out of a thousand babies reaches adulthood.

Not just the babies but adult sea turtles too are in constant danger from fishing nets and turtle hunters. Sounds bad, doesn't it? Well, it is. And that's why we were out on that January night to collect sea turtle eggs and take them to the hatchery, where they would be safe from human and animal predators. When the babies hatched two months later, we would put them back into the sea. We had been doing this for several years, and this time we had 30 nests already incubating (developing) in the hatchery.

The shiny round blob, weighing as much as a suitcase, lumbered up the beach, stopping every few steps. Turtles are not designed to walk but to swim, so by the time this one had hauled herself on to the dry sand, she was pretty tired. But there was no time to rest; she had to finish her nesting job and hurry back to her watery environment as soon as possible; breathing and moving on land is no fun for a marine animal.

So the mother turtle quickly gets down to her first task: finding a nesting place she feels happy about. This could have to do with temperature, humidity, and the texture of the sand. She also has to make sure it is above the tidal mark, so her eggs won't get washed into the sea. After a few minutes of crawling around and comically gulping in mouthfuls of air, she begins to dig her nest hole. The hind flippers, working alternately, scoop out and fling sand to the left and right, sometimes smacking us smartly in the face. After half an hour of panting and wheezing and digging, the hole is about 35 centimetres deep and she takes a brief rest before laying her eggs. Her lachrymal glands work overtime to wash the eyeballs clean of sand and dust, giving her a sad, tearful look.

Sitting beside her, we watched the 132 eggs fall into the nest hole, coming singly or in twos or threes. Shiny, white ping-pong balls, soft and bouncy. Then another short gap before she began the next stage of her job: filling the nest hole with sand. The hind flippers got into action again, working like bicycle pedals to sweep sand back into the nest. As she finished filling it, we marked the spot with a little flag we'd brought along. The reason for this will become clear later.

This was certainly not the first time we'd watched a sea turtle nesting. But the excitement and wonder were just as strong as the first time. There is something so amazing about this 100-million-year-old reptilian ritual.

The nest is now level with the beach, and the eggs cosily packed into the efficient sand incubator. Now

Ridley nesting

there starts a deep thumping rhythm, like a tabla. Tucking in her head, the turtle flings her weight from side to side 20 or 30 times, to pack the sand tight and make the nest waterproof and secure.

Mrs Ridley now does something smart. She moves over a bit to the right and then to the left, ruffling up the sand to make a couple of 'false nests' to fool predators. By messing up a large area of sand, she raises the survival chances of the eggs. It's not going to be easy for a predator to locate this one.

Yet, there's one predator sea turtles haven't been able to fool, and that is the animal called Man. During the nesting season, groups of turtle-egg poachers roam the beaches at night, carrying a stick with a long iron spike at one end. Spotting a sea turtle track, they follow it up the beach to the tip of the 'V' from where she has returned to the water. Jab, jab, jab with the iron spike and soon you feel the bunch of rubbery eggs and dig them out.

As the tired turtle waddled back to the ocean, stopping now and then to flop down for a rest, we began to dig next to our flag. After all the false-nesting activity it would have been difficult to find the eggs if we hadn't flagged the exact spot. Unfolding a long cotton 'egg bag' we transferred the eggs to it, putting in a little wet sand for cushioning. But not too much, because on some nights we would end up carrying back three or four nests and it got pretty heavy!

We were taking the eggs back to a turtle hatchery to re-bury them in the sand but in a fenced-in place, safe from human and animal predators. Over the years we had hatched, and released into the ocean, thousands of baby turtles. It was wonderful to watch them quickly swim away to their ocean home. But sadly, in spite of these efforts and those of many other turtle lovers, the olive ridley continues to decline and every year there are fewer and fewer nests on our beaches. The four other species found in India, the leatherback, hawksbill, green and loggerhead, share the same fate.

Sea turtles need all the help they can get. Many marine biologists and conservationists, as well as wildlife officials, protect and hatch the eggs, and release the hatchlings into the ocean. But there are still huge challenges. For example, when baby sea turtles hatch, they have to make their way to the sea using the light – and reflection – of the sun, moon and stars. Electric lights on the beach, from houses and hotels, confuse the little turtles' sense of direction and they begin a tiring and often fatal trek in the wrong direction, away from the sea. Getting caught in vegetation or some man-made construction, they dehydrate in the hot sun and die. On many turtle-friendly beaches around the world, beach lights are either switched off or dimmed during the nesting and hatching seasons, to help turtles find their way better. But the hotels and resorts on our coast, along the East Coast Road, haven't done this in spite of repeated requests. To them, business is more important than wildlife, and their clientele want

Leatherback turtle

Hawksbill turtle

beach parties with harsh lights and loud music; both deterrents to nesting turtles.

Another sea turtle issue to keep in mind is the incubation temperature. Many countries now have nurseries where sea turtle eggs are buried and hatched, and the hatchlings released into the sea. Nest holes are dug to the depth and width of the natural nests and eggs buried in them for the 60-day incubation period.

This is all well and good, but we need to keep in mind that it is the nest temperature, and not genes and chromosomes and all that stuff, that decides whether the baby is going to be a male or a female! To have a balanced, natural mix of males and females, the incubation temperatures must be very carefully controlled. Otherwise, you'll end up with an all-male or all-female population. Some naturalists even feel that it is better to let eggs be destroyed rather than risk this happening. No, say others, unless we continue with nurseries – and do the best we can – species after species will go extinct. Already, the population of the Kemp's Ridley may be down to less than 3,000 nesting females.

Apart from the satisfaction of trying to help protect the olive ridley, our turtle walks were wonderful in other ways as well. On a typical turtle night, we

Green turtle

Loggerhead turtle

would start walking around 10 p.m. and return in the small hours of the morning after an 8–10 kilometre egg-hunt. The moonlight on the water, the carpet of stars twinkling in the heavens and in the ocean, the awesome silence broken only by our soft footsteps and the watery thumping of the waves...these are great memories. Once, dead on our feet at two in the morning, we curled up in a fishing boat on a bundle of nets, safe from the strong sandy winds. A couple of hours' sleep, then the long walk back.

Often we would find sea creatures stranded by the tide, and carry them to the water's edge. Sting rays, jellyfish, eels, sea snakes. One night, we almost stepped on three hook-nosed sea snakes thrashing feebly in the sand, on the verge of suffocation. As in all species of sea snakes, the tails were flat; useful paddles for speedy ocean travel. Sea snakes are highly venomous, with no antivenom in India, so we handled them very carefully indeed, even though they are not aggressive and rarely bite. At that time, we had a large sea snake display at the Snake Park, so we decided to take them back with us. They were put in a bucket, which was made 'escape proof' with a canvas cover tied down with rope. However, it wasn't as secure as we'd thought. Switching on the bathroom light later that night, I almost stepped on one; two had managed to get out. There was much excitement in our household until they were re-arrested and imprisoned, this time in the high-security store room.

Several photographers and film-makers asked for our help in capturing nesting sea turtles on camera. We were happy to do this since it meant more publicity and sympathy for the plight of the olive ridley. They were fast becoming the rock stars of the reptile world in Chennai, with many newspapers and magazines publishing photos and articles about these beautiful females. One season, a German photographer almost got us killed when we met a group of egg poachers crouching near a turtle, collecting the eggs as she laid them.

This is a sight that makes the nature-lover's blood boil. Our friend began swearing loudly (luckily in German) and pulled out his penknife, threatening to take the poachers to the police unless they put back all the eggs. They returned the compliment, shouting and waving their spiked egg sticks in warrior-like fashion. Soon, they had supporters running out from a nearby fishing village. It was a sticky situation and we had to tell a lie to get out of it. This poor foreigner, we told them, was crazy, and didn't know what he was doing or saying. He was to be pitied, and forgiven. They took their eggs and went off, only half-convinced.

Another night we were with a film crew, driving along the beach in a jeep filled with equipment including long, gun-like cameras, tripods, lights and a generator. The driver had no experience in water's-edge navigation and kept going into the soft sand instead of keeping to the hard wet strip at the tidal line. Soon, of course, the tyres were nicely embedded, refusing to budge in spite of much pushing, shoving and shouting. To make matters worse, the tide was coming in. The wheels became half submerged and it looked like we would have to unload the equipment and let the jeep swim away into the ocean. It was a lonely stretch of beach and, anyway, at two in the morning it's not easy to find help. Fortunately, one final desperate push from all of us caused a small forward jump. Another heave brought it out of the deep ditch that the spinning wheels had created.

I became very interested in sea turtles. I read books and articles about them, and met sea turtle conservationists. Two of these were right in our midst: Satish Bhaskar and Valli. Satish had performed the amazing and slightly mad feat of living by himself on a small, uninhabited island in Lakshadweep for five months to study turtle nesting. A boat dropped him there, and promised to pick him up five months later. No electricity, little fresh water, no company, no phone or other communication. To add to the challenge, a huge dead whale shark was washed up on his beach, stinking up the whole island. Until a high tide washed it out to sea again, he had to live with the terrible smell.

Valli was no less adventurous. He was an ace turtle walker, and would cover miles and miles on nesting

Ridleys

nights, to bring back eggs to the hatchery. His reports have important and path-breaking observations and photographs of Indian sea turtles.

Keen to find out about the slaughter of sea turtles for meat, I visited the turtle market in Tuticorin. This was definitely one of the goriest and sickening sights I've seen. Hundreds of sea turtles – hawksbills, greens and ridleys – were lined up on the hot pavement, upside-down, thrashing helplessly. Being on land and in this unnatural position, they struggled to breathe and their mouths were open, gasping for air. When one was sold, the plastron or bottom shell was ripped off the turtle in one yank, leaving its intestines hanging out. It was chopped up, and the meat sold, while it was still alive; sometimes it took them over an hour to die.

In this part of Tamil Nadu it is believed that a drink of fresh sea turtle blood is good for the health. Turtle throats were being slit, and the blood collected in steel tumblers to be sold at two rupees. The customer would quickly gulp it down, before it coagulated. Meanwhile, the turtle slowly bled to death. It was animal cruelty at its height, and I think that the pictures we took and sent to the wildlife authorities helped stop this ghastly torture.

A much happier collection of sea turtles is at Gahirmatha beach in the Kendrapara district of Odisha. This is one of nature's chosen holy places, one of the sites of the '*arribada*'. This Spanish word means arrival. An *arribada* is when hundreds of thousands of sea turtles come ashore together to nest. It's one of those crazy animal scenes like the wildebeest migrations in Africa where animals are jostling and falling over each other for lack of space.

Sea turtle experts think that over 300,000 ridleys come ashore every year at Gahirmatha. The *arribada* happens over several nights, usually eight or ten, but that still means that thousands of turtles are nesting (or trying to nest!) on a short three-kilometre stretch of beach. One can hardly believe the crazy impossibility of the scene unless you've seen it. Females dig up each other's eggs to lay their own, climb over one another, and often just dump their eggs out in the open. The next morning, there is a stench of raw egg that may turn away the hungriest predator!

If I could live my life again, I would be a sea turtle biologist. What a fascinating group of animals – and so much yet to be discovered about them! Their migrations and travel – over thousands of miles of ocean – are still not completely clear to scientists in spite of years of study of tagged turtles. And – an important consideration – they don't bite and attack, which is a great advantage when studying animals. But since I'm not likely to live another life, I'll just enjoy my sea turtle memories. Scooping up baby turtles and putting them into the ocean is the happiest of these.

Froggy, Froggy

Froggy, froggy, in the pool,
You need to go to singing school;
You need to learn the notes again
So that your song is not in vain.

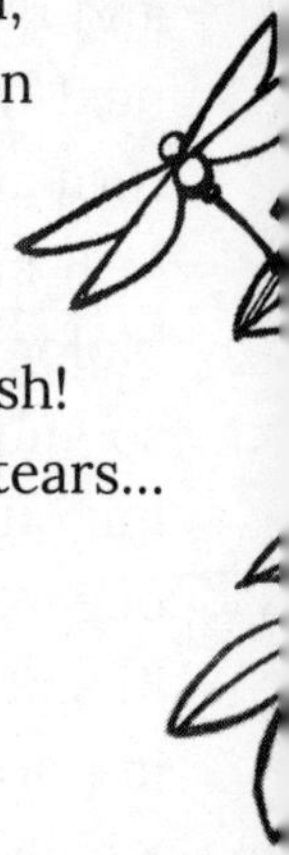

Froggy, froggy, in the marsh,
Your tunes are so extremely harsh!
Your symphony will bring forth tears...
Unless I quickly block my ears.

Froggy, froggy, in the lake,
How many verses will it take
For you to listen to my plea
And give up singing, totally?

Islands of Paradise

I am not a particularly adventurous person. But I ended up doing some pretty adventurous things, for one reason or the other. Quite often, I've found myself in a situation that, well, I simply shouldn't have been in. One day, for example, I found myself going off to the Andaman Islands on the rusty old ship *State of Haryana*, along with an Irular snake-hunter Anamallai.

The Andaman and Nicobar Islands are a treasure trove of reptile secrets and mysteries, and the Snake Park was keen on finding out about these. Sea snakes came up in their thousands to lay eggs on the beaches. Saltwater crocodiles that cruised its backwaters and lagoons grew so huge here that there were stories of attacks on humans, and even small boats. In the Nicobars, six-metre reticulate pythons lay across forest tracks looking like fallen tree trunks. There were flying snakes, and even king cobras, the longest venomous snakes in the world, and the only snakes that make a nest...and so in a weak moment I offered to go. Now here I was, on a four-day ocean trip with a very seasick Anamallai for company. And a few very bold rats as well, which raided my biscuits and fruit every night.

The Andaman-Nicobar archipelago of over 300 islands lies about 1,000 kilometres east of Chennai, in the Bay of Bengal. It is one of the most beautiful island chains in the world. Here, the tops of the trees tower 30 metres above the forest floor. Cool, clear streams flow through dense undergrowth. The coasts of the islands are fringed with beautiful mangroves, trees which grow in seawater and have strange, twisted roots. The sand is ice-white and makes a pearly ring around the islands. Beyond it, in the shallow waters, are coral reefs, one of nature's Aladdin's Caves: teeming with strange and wonderful plants and animals.

This rich range of island habitats, plus their geographical location – so close to Thailand and Indonesia – makes a great home for endemic species. Endemics are plants and animals that have evolved, for millions of years, in that one place, and are found nowhere else. They may have relatives; but at some point, ages ago, they began their own lonely evolutionary journey to fit their unique habitat.

Endemics are typical of islands but are also found on land 'islands', such as rainforests, which are different from the environment around. The high, forested mountains of the Western Ghats are an example. The Andamans and Nicobars have many fascinating endemics including frogs, birds, lizards, snakes and even mammals. We were sure that a study there would reveal new species; and over the years, during many collections and surveys, this has proved to be true.

For years, we had been reading old natural history reports about the inhabitants of this reptile haven. We also dived into moth-eaten old books in old, old library rooms, to learn about the fascinating history of the islands. I am sure that no other place has such a colourful and story-like history. Until recent years, there were still 'primitive' tribes in the Andamans – like the Jarawa – who lived in the jungle, eating only wild plants and animals, making fire, and tolerating no contact with the outside world. Things have changed dramatically and today there are just a few Andaman-Nicobar Adivasis who are living the old, peaceful life in the forest.

My assignment was to make contact with islanders who would help us in future studies: government officials, businessmen, people interested in natural history and conservation. I also hoped to collect a nest of saltwater crocodile eggs to hatch and rear in captivity. The Irular snake expert Anamallai and I were going to bring back any interesting reptiles we came across.

I began making friends with the people of the Andamans long before I got there. Sitting on the deck of the ship, watching the endless stretch of blue, blue water, I met the chief engineer who told me in a boastful tone how unseaworthy the *Haryana* was. She was too old, and would simply sink on one of these trips. 'Just rust, that's all there is to her,' he boomed. I pointed nervously at the lifeboats – wouldn't they...? No, no, he answered, they would go down with the ship because the rust had glued them permanently to the deck railings. 'No proper maintenance,' he explained needlessly. Well...life jackets...? Yes, but there was a small problem: there weren't nearly enough for all the passengers. Seeing my paling face, he added generously that he'd make sure I had one.

Talking to some of the colourful islanders was no less scary. They were returning to the islands after a holiday on the mainland. Each one had stories that either made your hair stand on end, or curl up immediately. One, a farmer, told me how three fishermen had been arrowed by the Jarawa while they were poaching fish in the Jarawa Reserve. A shark-fin exporter spoke of a shark attack that subtracted one of his nephew's arms.

There were amazing accounts of the six tribes that live in the Andamans and Nicobars: the Jarawa, Onge, Sentinelese, Shompen, Nicobarese and Andamanese. Of these, only the Sentinelese have some hope of a safe future, because we outsiders have left them alone on their small island of North Sentinel. All the others have been pushed off their traditional land into small pockets without enough fresh water, and are dying from the diseases which we expose them to. We, the 'civilized' and 'educated' outsiders, have killed off some of the most ancient and wonderful cultures in our country, from sheer greed and cruelty.

Others talked about the Japanese occupation of the islands during the Second World War, when thousands of people were murdered because they were suspected of being supporters of the British government. Groups of them were dumped on uninhabited islands with no food or water, and left there to starve to death. Later, in Port Blair, I visited the charming little Japanese Shinto shrine. Sitting on moss-covered stones in the beautifully designed garden, I thought about how cultures can be both so sensitive and so barbarian at the same time.

A fellow traveller, a fisherman from North Andaman, told me about his incredible luck. A couple of months ago, he was on an overnight camp in a small channel between two islands. Walking to one of the beaches at low tide, he found what islanders would give an eye – or at least a tooth – for: a large lump of ambergris. Ambergris is one of the richest natural treasures, like diamonds, sandalwood and gold. It is a substance that whales throw up; we don't quite know why or how or when. But it's worth its weight in gold in the perfume industry, because it's a 'fixer', and keeps a fragrance alive for a long time. This fisherman was now on his way back from mainland India, having sold his find, richer by a lakh or two. He spoke about building a house for his family, and sending his daughters to school and college. A nice true fairy tale. Once in a while, fairy tales actually happen.

However, a fairy tale of a different kind awaited me at Port Blair. 'Madam, your passport, please,' said a scary voice behind me. In those days, in the early 1970s, the Andamans were closed to foreigners unless they had a special permit from the Ministry of Home Affairs in New Delhi.

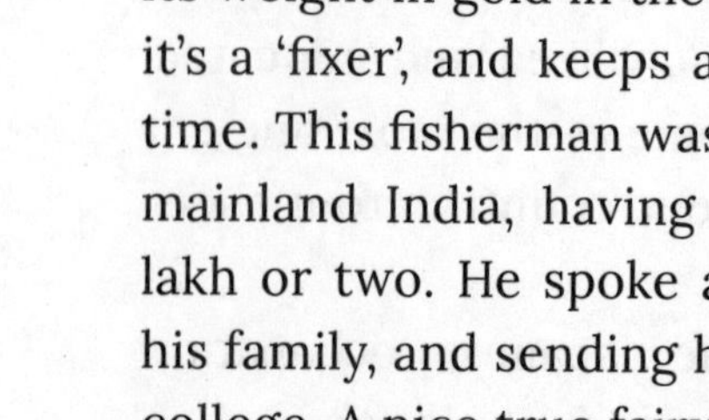

My shaky voice said, 'But I am an Indian citizen, I don't have to carry my passport, nor do I need a permit.'

'Madam, your name is Whitaker, that is not an Indian name.'

'This is my husband's name, but my passport is...' and so on, with poor results. Anamallai and I were soon trotting along to the police station, feeling very afraid and anxious.

There was no crime on the islands then, so the police force was bored and unoccupied, and very happy to have something to do. They asked me endless questions, wrote a long report and made long phone calls to one another in the same room. Then I did a brilliant thing, for once. I remembered an important name. Fred Burn. Fred was my uncle's ham (radio) buddy in the Andamans, the manager of the Wimco match factory in Port Blair. They 'chatted' to each other in Morse code about the weather, because practically every other topic was banned for national security reasons. When my uncle heard I was going to the Andamans, he phoned and asked me to look up Fred and report back on what he was like. 'I want to know,' he said, 'if he's as nice as he sounds.'

'I would like to make a phone call,' I told the large policeman who was now saying I'd have to take the ship back to Chennai the next morning, and cool my heels in the lock-up until then. More eager policemen had come in, and I was obviously providing useful employment. After some scary-sounding discussion, they allowed me to dial 247 which, if I remember correctly, was the Wimco factory number. Fred Burn was its manager at the time.

Within the next ten minutes, I was transported from hell to heaven. I stopped being a criminal, and became a VIP because Fred Burn, I discovered, was the King of the Andamans. When he appeared at the police station in his little old Fiat, the policemen's jaws dropped. When he declared that Saad Ali's niece was a friend and had to stay at Wimco Bungalow, the jaws dropped further. And when he hugged me and told Anamallai and me to get into the car with our knapsacks, I became royalty in their eyes. I tried not to smirk or gloat as we drove away...but couldn't resist a small (victorious) wave of the hand.

Fred and Jean Burn were ideal hosts. I had a large room overlooking the ocean, wonderful food and a running commentary on the history of the islands. I should have taped my conversations with them, because they knew more about this secret part of the world than all the history books can tell us.

Fred, who had a British father and a Burmese mother, had been the head of the Bush Police, set up by the British government to 'control' the tribes, specifically the Jarawa. It was the Jarawa territory that the British, and then the Indians, were encroaching on, pushing them further and further away from their traditional hunting and fishing grounds. Naturally, the Jarawa were upset, and retaliated in a 'hostile' way. But it was guns and other modern weaponry against bows and arrows, and hundreds of Jarawa had been massacred in this unfair and cruel tug-of-war over land and resources. Today, there may be less than 250 Jarawa left; and unless we respect their rights and culture, this tribe too will go the way of the Andamanese.

A few days later we were on the inter-island ferry boat *Cholunga*, on our way to North Andaman Island to look for crocodiles. We were lucky to meet two of the 20 or so surviving members of the Andamanese tribe. One of them was Loka, the headman, who had seen many sad changes in his long life. He'd seen his people change from lively, happy forest people to victims of 'civilization'.

Looking down into the depths of the ocean, I saw sea turtles, dolphins and fish as if under glass. For the next week, we based ourselves at the forest rest house in Diglipur and travelled along the hundreds of creeks, often from dawn till late into the night. As I said before, night-time 'shining' for crocodile eyes is the best way to count crocodiles, because their eyes produce a convenient bright glow. During the day, it's difficult because crocs hear well and go underwater at the slightest sound...and stay there. By slowing down their heartbeat, they can stay underwater, without breathing, for hours. This survival trick is called 'bradycardia'.

Sometimes the dungy – fishing boat – would get grounded in the shallows and we'd have to walk in the tidal slush, cutting our feet on the sharp mangrove roots. As if this wasn't enough, thousands of sandflies feasted on our arms and legs. Sandflies are invisible monsters. You can't see them, but they can see you. Their bites itch for as long as you keep scratching them. And it's impossible not to scratch, because they're just about the itchiest bites in the world.

However, apart from a pair of giant tracks – of a croc at least five metres long – we saw nothing. Poachers had finished off the once healthy population of saltwater crocodiles. One of these poachers, whom we met at the local tea shop, boasted of having killed 883 crocodiles. The skins were sent to the mainland

and brought in good money, because 'salties' have the most valuable skins of all crocodile species. We went home with him to see his various crocodile trophies. One of the skulls was a metre long. I begged from him a tooth as large as a pig tusk, which belonged to a seven-metre monster. 'It was a spirit crocodile,' the poacher said, 'and we had to spear, hook and shoot it several times before it died.' During the final struggle, he said, he fell into the croc's mouth! They had to get a crane to lift the animal and take it to Diglipur, where it was skinned.

When not being killed by sandflies on the creeks, we were in the forest looking for reptiles. On the first forest walk I was delighted to be away from sandfly country. I had read about the leeches of the Andamans, but they surfaced in the monsoon, and this was the dry

season. I was to discover, however, that both leeches and sandflies were better than what we got: thousands and thousands of little ticks. They itched more than sandflies. They started out tiny, hardly visible, and you woke up the next morning to find a large grey blob on your stomach, or arm, or ear. Yuck. They found the cosiest hiding places – between the toes, behind the ears – and waited it out for days; then, suddenly, bloated up with blood. I was picking ticks off myself after my return to Chennai over a month later.

Our specimen collection grew. It included several endemics like the Andaman day gecko and the Andaman cat snake. A krait we found dead on the road turned out to be a new species. Anamallai was in seventh heaven despite the ticks. And soon we were on the *Cholunga* once more, going south to Mayabunder on Middle Andaman Island. Mayabunder is the home of the Karens, a Myanmarese community known for its forest skills. A group of Karens were brought over to the Andamans by the British in the early 1900s to clear the forest.

It was with the Karens that I first went into the coral reefs. They were diving with home-made snorkels and masks – for *Turbo* and *Trochus* shells, which are used to make buttons and trinkets. They were also collecting the strange-looking sea cucumbers for export to Singapore, where they are a great delicacy. The magic world of the reef is something everyone should get a chance to see. As we swam along lazily over large, lumpy coral beds, the water was filled with weird and wonderful shapes and colours. Bright orange sea anemones, green and purple bivalve shells, pulsating jellyfish, and millions of tiny zippy fish of every colour under or over the sun. Once in the reef, you are immersed in and become part of a wonder-world. When you come out, you can't quite believe you saw what you saw.

In the forests, more ticks, and more fascinating animals. One morning I went with a hunting party looking for water monitors; the meat is a treat in the islands and packs of trained hunting dogs know where to find them. No blue-blooded foxhound could have been a better hunter than these scrawny mongrels. On smelling a monitor, they set up an unholy yapping and fanned out in expert military fashion to corner their prey. The lizard was kept at bay until the hunters came and captured it.

It was in these forests that we found an Andaman cat snake, which is considered blind (its Hindi name is *andha saamp*) and highly venomous. We were seen as courageous heroes for handling this 'deadly' creature! That's the nice thing about snakes: they turn us ordinary, colourless people into celebrities.

Allen, my Karen guide and friend, and his cousins would often go to the edge of the Jarawa Reserve for pig, monitor and fish, because that's where the best hunting grounds were. But you had to be careful, because the Jarawa are sharp shooters, and one arrow is all you need. Many of the Karens, however, even risked going right into the reserve. About a year before my trip, a group of Karens went diving for *kloe-suchhi* (*Trochus* shells) on Mowar Tikri, a small island within the reserve. That night as they cooked their fish catch for dinner, the Jarawa must have seen them, and decided to take action.

At dawn, an arrow came flying through the air, swift and straight, right into the chest of one of the Karen intruders. The others realized immediately what was happening, and rushed to their dungy, anchored offshore in the shallows. But the Jarawa charged and kidnapped one of the party...he has never been heard of again. There is much guessing about whether he is alive and living in the reserve among the Jarawa.

Over the next 25 years, our Andamans team made many visits to the islands and had many adventures.

They found unreported sea turtle and sea snake nesting beaches, discovered new species of reptiles, caught king cobras and met wonderful people from the so-called hostile tribes. For all of us who loved these islands and their fantastic wildlife and people, it was a magic place where the 'real world' and its problems could be forgotten. Unfortunately, the last 20-30 years have brought disastrous changes in spite of the efforts of many committed conservationists.

Me, the Great Birdwatcher

I come from a family of ornithologists, or birdwatchers. This is an eccentric bunch of people who wake up while all sensible people are sleeping, fill water bottles and go off to spend the day in the hot sun looking for birds. They often miss meals in the excitement of chasing a bird and get quite irritable if it flies off without being seen properly. They make lists of birds they've seen that day and get annoyed if someone has seen more. They don't like it if someone sits on their binoculars by mistake, or drops them: both things that I was unlucky enough to do. They can't just enjoy the sight of a pretty bird. No; they must learn its name, distribution, habits, food, and other more personal details. I'm sure birds don't like this kind of nosiness at all. I mean, how would *you* like someone studying you all the time?!

Well, as I said, my family were all bird nuts. While other (normal) families went to the movies or Sunday barbecues, I was dragged off to the Borivali National Park (also known as Sanjay Gandhi National Park). 'Just think!' my father would say excitedly. 'We might hear the call of the white-crested cuckoo!'

Since we had to be out of the house by six or sometimes earlier, preparations were made the night before. Binoculars were lovingly spat on and cleaned, bird books located and fought over, pencils sharpened. (A proper birdwatcher writes notes with a pencil, not a pen). I heard my mother call for our cook Paul and listened intently to find out the menu for the picnic. My heart sank when I heard the words, 'Make some sandwiches, Paul, for tomorrow morning.' Because Paul's sandwich sums were always a bit wrong. He believed that six people could live on eight sandwiches. I slipped a few toffees into my skirt pocket, to keep myself alive during the ordeal.

Still, waking up early and then starving to death were small issues. I could deal with them. The real challenge was hiding my ignorance. Often, there were others along as well, friends or relatives, and everyone expected me to be just as clever as the rest of my family, and to know all the names and addresses of the birds we saw. I had to pretend to be a 'birder'. Also,

Sálim Mamoo, our uncle and famous ornithologist, was often along and he got very upset if you didn't recognize some bird flying about ten thousand miles above your head. Yet another problem for me was that my sister was a very good birdwatcher and often knew the names of birds the others didn't. So how could I be left out? How could I allow our guests to find out that I was the dunce of the family? Over the years, I developed certain tricks which I will now share with you. Who knows? You may find yourself in a similar situation, and I feel it's my duty to help anyone who is in the kind of tight spot I was in.

Rule Number One: Don't try to fight this birdwatching disease. It's impossible. For a birdwatcher, birds are the only important thing in the world. They are interested in nothing else. Neither can they understand how, or why, a person can be uninterested (or less interested than they are) in birds. They will climb trees, walk ten miles in mud, go without food and water for days, in the hope of seeing some silly little brown bird. So just leave them alone. They are beyond help.

Number Two: It's important to look like a birdwatcher, and binoculars are a useful crutch. Always have them around your neck. Binocs immediately mark you as part of the group and establish your identity as

a 'birder'. As the birdwatching trip starts, play with the focus thing with a slight frown, a puzzled look. The reason for this will become clear later.

Number Three: If there's food along, pretend you're not interested in it. Pretend that food simply isn't important. Once in a while, even suggest a picnic isn't necessary at all. This is difficult, I know, but it creates a good impression. It gives the others the feeling that you rate birds above sandwiches and cookies.

Number Four: Soon enough, the moment will come when a sorry brown object flies across the path or croaks from a tree. The birders stop, electrified. 'What was that?' they ask, looking in your direction. Binocs go up, mouths fall open, someone is looking at you hopefully, waiting for an opinion. Don't give it. If it's the wrong name, and it probably would be, then you've had it. Blame your binocs. And this is where the focus knob comes in. Twiddle it and look disturbed. Look as if you'd have loved to see the bird but can't because of the silly binoculars. And let me repeat: keep your mouth shut. If you excitedly shout out a name, your grave is dug. It may well be a bird that's off migrating in Siberia, or extinct, or simply non-existent.

Number Five: Every now and then, snatch up your binocs excitedly, and glare and squint fiercely at a tree. Stand absolutely still for at least 50 seconds.

Then relax, shrug, and say, 'Oh, it's only a babbler.' Or some other common bird, like sparrow, or parakeet, or bulbul. This exercise has a double advantage. It tells the others that you know your stuff, and also that you are above these common and uninteresting babblers and bulbuls.

Number Six: Avoid going with the same birding group twice. Once is plenty. Fooling them once is entirely possible, but twice is stretching it. Sooner or later, one gets found out and, believe me, it isn't pleasant. And – this is important – make sure that you never go out with just one person, because this puts a huge burden on you. Your ignorance has a better chance of getting neutralized in a large group. The more, the better.

Number Seven: Quick thinking is a must. Let me give you an example. The other day, someone asked me the difference between two species of laughing thrushes: the Nilgiri and the Palani. I chuckled and said, 'Oh, I'm not one of those finicky birdwatchers.' See that? I managed to hide the fact that both thrushes are total strangers to me.

Well, that's the end of my list, and good luck to you. But I must add another example of how I have managed to survive in the frightening world of birdwatchers. A few years ago, I was in Minnesota in the United States. My hosts, friends of my parents, decided to take me birdwatching 'as a special treat'. Ouch. They even lent me a superb pair of binoculars, newly serviced and powerful as a telescope. I felt miserable and helpless. Now, I thought, my secret is sure to be out.

We turned off the highway on to a dirt track, which led to a lovely lake. Just then a bunch of noisy objects flew across the road. 'Isn't it a bit early for the Canada geese?' I asked David. They were both impressed. They hadn't noticed the small signboard, with a picture, that we had just passed. I, on the other hand, had. And so we come to *Rule Number Eight*: Keep your eyes peeled.

The Zoo Tiger

Yusuf was excited, and when he was excited, he couldn't sit still. When he couldn't sit still, he jumped around and banged into things. When he banged into things, those stupid things broke. And when those stupid things broke, Amma, for some strange reason, got angry. So far, he had broken two teacups, a small lamp and the crystal bottle given by the Russian telephone people to Papa. So Amma screamed at Yusuf a total of four times. But it didn't matter to Yusuf...much. Because this was a special time. Birthday. A time he had been waiting for. Zoo time. Tomorrow. He had made Amma and Papa repeat the schedule again and again, like a song.

'We'll take the 8 o'clock bus to Trivandrum,* visit the tiger, have lunch at a hotel and come back home.'

**Now Thiruvananthapuram*

The hotel meal was going to be a big treat all right, no doubt about that, but definitely, the best was the tiger. The thought of those two treats together – the lunch and the tiger – was almost unbearably exciting. The four crashes and four scoldings were all the tiger's fault.

It was difficult to eat dinner that night, because all the space in Yusuf's stomach was occupied by excitement. And Amma was on one of her health trips, so they had sprouted beans and yoghurt and that sort of thing. Yusuf comforted himself by imagining the hotel food in store for him the next day. 'Come on – eat, boy, or we'll have to cancel the birthday treat. Tigers don't like skinny boys.' Every year for Yusuf's birthday, Papa made one or two jokes. Then it was a humour drought till the next birthday.

His birthday was also a time for some democracy in an otherwise autocratic household government. Yusuf could choose what he wanted to do on that day. Last year, he had asked for a boat ride. What a stupid choice! Was he mad! But then that was before he saw 'The Land of the Tiger' on the *National Geographic* channel.

Actually, he hadn't seen the whole film because that evening he had four or five hours of homework. But he'd seen one shot of the tiger jumping across a dry riverbed, and that was enough. It was like magic, like a spirit, like a bolt of orange lightning. The wild, bright power of the animal filled Yusuf's imagination and for many days there was no space in his mind for anything else. It was the most exciting experience of his life. It was like a dream...come true.

So that's why he chose the zoo visit for his birthday. He wanted to revisit the dream. He wanted to glimpse that shining sunset gleam on the animal's coat as every movement brought a heavy ripple of muscles.

The birthday morning began when Papa came in to wake him up and do his birthday act. 'What? Do I see some lumpy object under the bed? Did Ramraj forget to clean under the bed or what?'

Smiling, half asleep still, Yusuf opened the three packages. A bright blue pencil case with everything already inside, including one of those new kinds of pencils that you could sharpen on the pencil cap. A sun hat with a Velcro clasp, with Los Angeles written all over it. The latest *Limca Book of Records.*

A good loot. As usual Amma quickly took away the wrapping paper for future use and Papa started his lecture about looking after these precious new things properly. 'You know we are not rich, and yet we try to...'

'Yes-yes, Papa, I know.' On birthdays, you could even tell your parents to be quiet.

Breakfast, special shoes, shouting goodbye to the house, almost breaking a plate, and then they were at the bus stop and, soon after, on a bus. Window seat, to cap it all. Yusuf spent the half-hour bus ride trying to imagine how it would be – seeing a real tiger. He began a letter in his head to his grandmother, describing the visit and the tiger. How do I describe that shine, that confidence, the pride (almost boastfulness) of the animal? Granny must be told, of course. And he worked away at the letter, because Malayalam and English got mixed up in his head and he had to sort out some of the words.

The zoo entrance, the ticket booth, the candyfloss – whoever would want candyfloss, for heaven's sake? – the slight bustle, the which-way-do-we-go. Reading the signs pointing to different animals. Bear, hyena, elephant, this way. Tiger...

'What shall we do, Yusuf? Tiger first?'

Of course not. The tiger should come last. Yusuf didn't have to speak; his face said it.

So they began meandering around, like typical zoo families. They spent almost an hour at the monkey cages because they were being fed, and there was one naughty baby whose mother was trying to groom it. But the baby kept running away from her and defying her with squeaky chattering. For a while, the mother played along, pretending she couldn't catch it and the baby was winning. Then she suddenly got serious, the way mothers do, grabbed the tiny head and began snatching at lice or fleas or whatever there was.

It was about noon when they came to the tiger cage. Papa was there first and called out to Yusuf to hurry up. 'Come, quick, he's right next to the bars, you can get a good view.'

Panting with excitement, Yusuf went up the little slope where Papa was standing, peering at the bars of the cage.

It was a big male and it lay with its length along the cage, which was only a little bigger than he was. He was facing away from them, and when Papa poked him with a stick, he gave a low, hoarse cough of protest but didn't bother to get up. Flies buzzed around his head and on the meat chunks that lay on the cage floor. Crows feasted on the meat and didn't seem at all scared of the king of the jungle. His coat was not shiny, but dull and rough like an unbrushed carpet.

Yusuf walked over to the other side and saw that one eye was closed and swollen. The bones showed like the angles of a badly made cardboard cut-out. The stench made you want to puke. Yusuf walked away down the path, his head hot and churned up.

Papa was calling out to him. 'Come, we'll poke it, it will get up. What's the matter with you?'

Yusuf lost control. He lost the correct words too, and couldn't explain. 'It's not what I wanted! It's not the same animal! Don't poke it, don't stand there, let's go home! I want to go home!' The shouting grew louder and Amma and Papa, confused, looked at each other helplessly. 'Well, let's go and have lunch then,' said Papa.

Yusuf didn't want lunch. He just wanted to go home, away from the zoo, away from the tiger. As they left, the sick tiger made a weak swipe at a crow sitting on its back. But the crow knew it had found a safe perch, and didn't move.

Saviours of the Sky Islands

The Western Ghats are one of our geographical celebrities. This mountain range is among the world's 35 biodiversity hotspots, which is a big honour. But it doesn't stop there; they are also one of the eight 'hottest' of the hotspots. Further, they've won yet another ecology-Grammy: the Western Ghats, or Sahyadris, are a UNESCO World Heritage Site!

The Palani Hills (actually mountains) are one of the stars of the Western Ghats, a treasure trove like no other. Apart from their rich biodiversity, the Palanis have wildlife corridors to neighbouring mountain ranges, and two unique ecosystems.

The first one, the sholas, are cloud forests that nestle in the valleys. With many endemic species that are found nowhere else, these forests are rich in biodiversity. The second are the montane grasslands. These habitats are just as important as the sholas: maybe even more so, because they retain rainwater, which then flows down and is used by communities on the plains. This mountain mosaic, of peaks, valleys, sholas, grasslands, and plateaus (like Kodaikanal) is called a sky island. Sky islands are isolated mountains surrounded by very different habitats. They are fantastically beautiful, and the views are simply breathtaking. I went to Kodaikanal in 1987 for a short stay, and stayed for 18 years! The Palani Hills bug had bitten me, good and proper.

It also bit Bob Stewart and Tanya Balcar, two British backpackers who were travelling through southern India in 1985. They decided to do a short Kodai visit, and 'take in' the mountains. Three decades later, they were still there. They had become an important part of Kodai's conservation community, and their commitment to wildlife and its habitat was phenomenal. Their deaths – Tanya's in 2016, and Bob's four years later – left a huge vacuum. They died too soon, too young, but left a legacy of immense value: an ecological understanding of the Palani ecosystem. This will help conserve and restore it. It's an interesting story with a funny twist. It's also a reminder that things aren't always what they seem!

In 1852, a British army officer, Major Partridge, made a grave ecological error. He introduced three exotic plants – eucalyptus, pine and Australian wattle – to the Palanis. No doubt a well-meant attempt to provide fuel for the 'natives', it was disastrous for the environment. These exotic species quickly changed the fragile montane ecosystem. With none of their natural checks and controls, exotic plants tend to go mad, spreading like wildfire and wiping out indigenous species.

At that time, people were ignorant about the importance of montane grasslands as natural water systems. They called them wastelands; and these were planted with Major Partridge's exotics. The plantations were 'successful', bringing in money, timber and firewood. This plantation practice continued after Independence. Truckloads of timber and fuel wood hurtled down the mountain tracks to Kodaikanal, and towns and cities on the plains. It caused a serious loss of the grasslands and shola forest, a precious ecosystem that is the source of most of the big south Indian rivers.

This was the sad situation when forest-loving Bob and Tanya arrived in Kodai (and the reason they never left). They set to work. Using their small savings, they started a shola nursery in the garden of their rented cottage in Vattakanal: three greenhouses with fruit and fuel species for distribution, and hundreds of shola species, many grown for the first time ever. Ornamental cacti were also cultivated, for sale to hotels and resorts; the income from this helped maintain the nursery.

Thus started a shola restoration project that brought high praise and appreciation. Bob and Tanya involved youngsters from the local community, and formed the Vattakanal Conservation Trust. Thousands of seedlings were distributed free, and new data collected on the seeding, germination and care of shola plants. They worked closely with the Tamil Nadu Forest Department and NGOs like the Palani Hills Conservation Council.

However, there was a missing piece, a crucial one. They wanted to re-plant the sholas, and applied for permission from the Forest Department. But these are Protected Areas, and it took a long time, and many meetings. Finally, the precious letter arrived – the permission to enter and work in the sholas. Bob and Tanya began a botanical feat: hard physical activity, meticulous record keeping, and managing their growing army of young volunteers.

They were doing something no one had done before. They were growing forests in their nursery and putting them back in the sholas. To those of us lucky enough to have seen them in the field, their knowledge of plants was stunning. They would rattle off the name of the most insignificant little grassy tendril or liana on a mossy trunk. They identified and rescued many rare plants through this grow-and-plant technique. Pambar shola was one of their conservation sites. How thrilled they were, when expert botanists couldn't tell the difference between the original, 'natural' parts of the shola and the ones they had restored! Or when Nilgiri langurs returned to a patch they had grown. This raised hopes that one day the Nilgiri pipit, locally extinct, would be heard again in the montane grasslands. There were regular long, steep walks to and from Marion, Blackburn, Picnic and other shola forests. There were leeches and nettles. There was much 'bum-sliding' on steep, slippery slopes during the rains.

One early morning in May 2014, the Palanis conservation community was delighted to see this headline in the *Hindu* newspaper: 'State Prepares to

Eliminate "Aliens" from Rainforests'. The Court had asked the Forest Department of Tamil Nadu to remove the exotic plantations, which were endangering the forests and grasslands of the Western Ghats. To us, the Kodai community, it seemed as if there was finally a glimmer of hope for the shola-grassland mosaic of our magic mountains. Some of us had been viciously uprooting acacia saplings while on hikes and picnics, feeling like courageous environmental activists. We waited for more news on this plantation-elimination initiative. The government bureaucracy was gearing up to eradicate the plantations. The scale of the project would be enormous.

In the meantime, while walking along the edge of Blackburn Shola, Bob and Tanya had made an important botanical discovery. They spied some

orchids growing on an old, mangled wattle tree, one of the exotic plantation species. They were seeing more and more of this evidence of the shola invasion of plantations. More importantly, they were also seeing how quickly the exotic species re-grew, when they were cut. Clear felling led to an explosion of weeds, and thousands more seedlings of the plantation species. Felling and clearing did not perform the magic of bringing back the sholas and grasslands. These findings were presented at workshops in Bangalore* and elsewhere, including the landmark symposium 'Forest Plantations and Biodiversity Conservation', which was attended by botanists and ecologists from several organizations in India and abroad. Bob and Tanya's findings were accepted and valued.

Their discovery changed the Palanis conservation movement, sort of turned the tables. These old plantations were actually shola nurseries! Of course, they shouldn't have been planted in the first place; but their removal at this stage would not help, and could even finish off the remaining grasslands and sholas.

Those of us who knew them, and their commitment to the Palanis, are hoping that the Kodaikanal

**Now Bengaluru*

township will build a memorial to these two outstanding botanists, who saved the sky islands of the Palanis. Yes, I call them botanists, though neither had any academic training in the subject, and none of the 'qualifications' we hold so dear. Rest in peace, Bob and Tanya, in your own, well-earned sky island; hopefully with a Nilgiri pipit trilling in the distance, and surrounded by the rare shola plants that will now survive, thanks to you.

(With thanks to Ian Lockwood for providing crucial resources for this article, and for reading the draft.)

Author's Note

Hello, Reader!

I hope you enjoyed reading *Cobra in My Kitchen and Other Adventures with Wildlife*. I really enjoyed writing it. It took me back to the days when life was one big adventure. We led such an unusual life, and were surrounded by strange creatures, both animal and human. Reptiles are funny animals to work with; they are fairly brainless but do rather smart things. I was lucky to be the wife, assistant snake catcher, cook, and general dogsbody of Rom Whitaker for 20 years. Rom is known as the Snake Man of India, with good reason. Put him anywhere – in a forest, desert, mountain, canyon – and he'll dive under something and come up with a snake in his hand. Often, this wasn't a very comfortable situation for me, or for our children.

I grumbled a lot... After all, who likes having a python loose in the house? Or a cobra wandering about in the kitchen? But it was also a lot of fun. There are some chapters about the animals we worked with, such as sea turtles and crocodiles. The hope is that you, the reader, become interested in the world of Indian natural history. It is fascinating, strange, and... fast disappearing.

When you are lucky enough to have the kinds of experiences I've had, it's only fair to share them with others. That's why I wrote this book. I have added some stories and poems for variety.

Heartfelt thanks to Hachette editor Vatsala Kaul Banerjee for having taken on this project and for her wonderful editing and organizing skills...and all the many other skills that go into the making of a book (such as tolerating a cranky author). And to everyone who features in these essays, stories and poems, for having given me such an exciting life!

A big thanks and hug to my son Nikhil for helping me with 'Turtles and Tortoises'. He corrected some really silly mistakes I'd made.